A Bride for the Aldonian King

An Aldonia Royals Novel

Kristine Lynn

A Bride for the Aldonian King
An Aldonia Royals Novel #2
Copyright © 2021 Kristine Lynn
All rights reserved.

ISBN (ebook) 978-1-953335-88-3
(print) 978-1-953335-89-0

Inkspell Publishing
207 Moonglow Circle #101
Murrells Inlet, SC 29576

Cover art by: Fantasia Frog Designs
Edited by: Audrey Bobek

To Isabel, my little love, my biggest adventure.

KRISTINE LYNN

CHAPTER ONE: THE GIRL

A paralyzing scream tore through Lorelai's otherwise calm walk of the stables. Her legs erupted in goosepimples, then acted on autopilot, propelling her with a purpose beyond feeding the horses.

Someone was in her barn.

With my horses.

Another peal of terror ripped through the air, lighting a fire in her chest. The same fear she'd shoved aside since her father's heart attack—fear her world was close to teetering off course—fueled the blaze.

Adrenaline coursed through her, sending her pulse north of one-eighty. She dropped the bag of feed from her shoulder, letting it *thump* in the dirt, and took off like the Devil was at her heels. The stable staff wasn't due to arrive for another week, so whoever was in the barn definitely shouldn't be.

From the sounds of things, they'd figured that out, too.

When she whipped around the corner, she froze as she took in the scene in front of her, too surprised to say or do anything but watch. A bubble of giddiness rose up her throat, but she choked back the laugh that could easily have turned into a sob of relief.

No one was hurt.

Just a young girl—maybe toddler was a better word—atop Lorelai's shoeing stool, stretched out on her tiptoes in scuffed black mary janes, her arm arched up and over the top of the cherry wood stall door that housed Lorelai's chestnut mare, Billie Jean. Billie Jean gave a palm-to-finger lick of the child's hand, eliciting another stomach-curdling scream followed by a fit of giggles.

Relief flooded Lorelai's system, purging the fear that lay dormant, waiting for the opportune time to rear its ugly head again. She needed to get a handle on that, and quick. She couldn't run her own hunting operation if she was crippled by fear every third minute. And she would run her own hunting operation—she'd see to that. Otherwise, what was she doing back here in a place riddled with memories that haunted her around every corner?

Speaking of things she needed to get figured out, ascertaining the identity of her secret stowaway was in order. But not just yet. The girl was having too much fun for Lorelai to jump in and spoil it too soon. She observed the child and horse together for a full three minutes, biting back a laugh each time the horse's tongue made contact with the girl, who squealed with joy. It was darn near the cutest thing Lorelai had ever seen. It was also an all-too-familiar sight, down to the tight auburn curls that fell down the back of the eager child. Lorelai's stomach lurched as she realized who the young girl reminded her of—herself.

She shut her eyes against the unrequested barrage of memories that assaulted her. The sounds of the horses as they snorted, whinnied, and chomped their food caused her heart to seize, adding to the threat of the images dancing at the back of her lids.

Her father reaching down, his brown eyes filled with love, passing off a salt lick for her to give the ponies when she wasn't much older than this girl.

His hands spanning the width of her waist as he lifted her atop her first horse, Winny.

Walking her through the pasture, describing his duties—hers now—as he squeezed her hand with excitement.

The rough working-man's skin of his hand on hers still tickled after all these years.

She let out a sigh riddled with guilt and love both.

If he were alive, he'd love this scene taking place in his old barn. Another young girl betrothing herself to the animals, to their care. Her heart threatened to beat out of her chest thinking about her father, about the barn and man who had raised her within its four walls. She cleared her throat, swallowing her past back into the pit of her chest where it belonged.

There would be time to mourn, but not yet. Not if she wanted to make a name for herself in the hunting community and get out from under the grief that washed over her like a rogue wave every time her father's face stormed her thoughts.

Forcing the issue, the girl let out a screech as she tumbled off the stool, landing on her backside, silk skirt and tulle petticoat up around her waist. Lorelai rushed to her side just as a solitary tear slipped down the girl's cheek, Lorelai's memories of her father all but forgotten for now.

"I'm okay," the girl huffed, standing up and brushing the red dirt from her dress with one hand, swiping at the tear with the other. She was all defiance and sass wrapped in the most precious package Lorelai had ever seen. In that way, she and the girl were different as night and day. She hadn't worn dress shoes outside of the Christmas pageant her father dragged her and Gregory to each year and not since, either.

No, she was a stable girl, through and through—no time or energy for frills in her life.

Lorelai didn't have the heart to tell the child not to

bother with the dress, that this particular dirt would be impossible to get out of that particular fabric. Too many rich and entitled young women had stained their finest silks and sweaters on the same crimson dirt when they stole down to the barn hoping for a glimpse of one of the princes during Lorelai's youth. Ha! It had served them right as far as Lorelai was concerned. You either came to the stables to ride or shouldn't come at all. Princes weren't an acceptable excuse to invade her and her father's work.

The small child didn't fall into the entitled category as she clearly was too young to know any better, but if she came back, Lorelai would make sure she did so in appropriate clothing. *If* she came back. This fragmented thought begged the question of why she was there in the first place. Something to consider, especially as no adult seemed to be missing the sweet girl.

"I see that. I also see you met Billie Jean. Would you like to pet her?" She may as well have offered the girl a pony of her own the way the girl's crystal-blue eyes gazed up at her, her smile full and bright, save the gap between her front two teeth. She nodded, her chin touching her chest with each dip of her head.

Lorelai opened the gate and showed the child how to hold her hand out for Billie Jean to smell her, to get comfortable around the strange, tiny being. Suddenly, she was her father, instructing a younger version of herself how to love the horses in a way that built a long-term relationship. It was the greatest gift he'd given her, and now she passed it on. How great was that?

Her throat constricted with the loss she was forced to relive now that she was back home. *Home.* Strange that word was no longer tied to the States as it was the past decade. Maybe it never had been; maybe her heart had never left the homeland that had shaped her into the woman she was today. She shook her head free of the persistent and relentless memories nagging at the back of her mind and gazed down at the little girl.

"What's your name, sweetie?" she asked.

The girl didn't break eye contact with the mare, a rarity in children these days from what Lorelai had gathered. Most of them couldn't keep their attention on a single thing for more than a hot minute. She blamed technology, the lack of getting out and getting dirty, riding bikes and horses compounded by the prevalence of devices as stand-in babysitters, parents even. She hated to think of what kids were missing out on. She'd never let tech raise her kids. If she ever had any, that was.

This one in front of her brought forth an ache from her abdomen in the form of a deep-seated wish she'd had a mother to pass down those instincts. She wouldn't trade her childhood for anything, but that didn't mean she couldn't think about what it had cost her to get it.

"I'm Ginny. I'm gonna be four. Can BillieJean come to my birthday party?"

Lorelai stifled another laugh that built in her chest, bubbled up her throat. The last thing she wanted to do was let the poor girl think she wasn't being taken seriously, but what a darling request. One that could never happen, of course. Not this horse. Not that kind of party.

Lorelai had a fleeting thought of Billie Jean all dolled up in a matching skirt and petticoat, little black loafers painted on her hooves, a silver party hat giving her the likeness of a unicorn, and smiled. It would be funny to see if it wouldn't end in disaster. Billie Jean wasn't exactly a patient horse. Nor was she as young as she used to be.

Lorelai felt the same about herself and cringed inwardly.

"It's nice to meet you, Ginny. You know, Billie Jean doesn't usually like being around kids, so I'm not sure she'll be a good horse to invite to your party, but guess what?"

"What?"

"That makes you extra special since she likes you."

"I like her, too."

"So, what brings you to my barn, Ginny?"

Ginny seemed to give that question some thought, her head tossed to the side, tight, chestnut curls cascading over her right shoulder. Finally, she shrugged, sending the curls rolling down her back.

"I'm waiting for my daddy. He works here."

He worked there? Whose daughter she might be, then?

Ginny hadn't mentioned a mother, so she could be one of the stable hands' daughters. They didn't typically bring spouses during hunting season since they worked fourteen-hour days and the boarding rooms were shared bunks. Except none of the new hands were boarded yet, and not one had mentioned bringing a child. Not that Lorelai would have minded, but the days were too busy, too sporadic to accommodate the needs of a child not yet in primary school, especially without a spouse to help out. That, and Ginny's clothes didn't exactly scream "stable kid."

So, she was a mystery. A well-dressed and even better-mannered mystery. The only clue Lorelai had were the crystalline eyes the color of the sky above her that gazed up at her now.

Lorelai's imagination conjured those pale-blue eyes on a man just a few years older than her, wondered what they must look like deep-set in a tanned face, complementing a square jaw. Maybe some stubble. Except she didn't need to push her imagination too far; she knew exactly what that man would look like since he'd haunted her dreams for more than a decade.

When *his* face entered her thoughts as if called from the depths, Lorelai pushed it back down aside the fear and haunting memories of her past that he was most certainly part of.

No time for that mess.

"Can I ride her? Please, please, please?" Ginny asked, drawing Lorelai out of her embarrassing daydream. The girl finally looked up from the mare to give Lorelai the most effective puppy-dog-eyed pleading look she'd ever witnessed. Lorelai laughed, unable to keep it at bay any longer. The truth was, she and Billie Jean were a lot alike. Lorelai didn't normally like kids either, but something about Ginny had her eating from the young girl's palm.

Those eyes. It was her eyes that held Lorelai captive beyond the general adorableness of the foreign creature. The powder-blue orbs, like a cloudless sky on a summer day, were as familiar as the barn was to her. How many times had she gazed into them on a man just older than her, in that same place, hoping to see love for her reflected back? The connection, the similarity between the eyes gazing up at her from her past and Ginny's staring at her now was as unnerving as her father's ghost haunting her around every corner of the barn that raised her. But it was impossible. That man didn't live here anymore.

And a good thing, too. She didn't think her heart could go full-force toward her dreams if he was there to distract her.

"Not today, but maybe at some point, I can take you two out in the arena."

"Did you hear that, BillieJean? We can ride in the *rena* someday."

Lorelai couldn't pull her gaze from the young girl as she talked to Billie Jean like they were old friends, running her hands down the thick hide of the mare. She especially loved the way Ginny said the horse's name like it was one word, *BillieJean*. Ginny was a perfect horse-obsessed clone of herself at that age. Physically, though, she more closely resembled the blue-eyed boy who'd been dear to Lorelai once, even though he hadn't known Lorelai even existed. Or worse, had considered her a pest the way she lusted after him from afar.

Ugh. She might have been a pest back then, but no more. If she ever saw him again, she'd, she'd…

Well, she didn't know what she'd do, only that her pining days were over where Robert of Puruse was concerned.

Lorelai shook her head loose of more memories that surfaced, frustrated that after all this time, all her successes, she couldn't get *him* out of her head. She'd moved to New York, earned her master's and doctorate degrees, but thinking of him sent her back to the days when she was merely Gregory's younger sister.

Well, she was so much more than that, now, and if he deigned to make the trip back to his childhood home, he'd find out just how much more. She just wished she didn't see him everywhere, like in the eyes of a strange girl in her barn.

"Ginny, I don't mean to rush you, but I've got a lot to get done before my staff gets here next week. Where does your daddy work? Or is your mommy around?"

The truth was, she'd rather let Ginny play with Billie Jean the rest of the afternoon, but the mare and her boarding mate needed to stretch their legs, get used to the thinner air up in the mountains. She owed them a good, long ride. Plus, she still had to muck the stalls and she didn't want to be out there past happy hour. New York had given her a lust for a long day capped off by a tall drink, preferably a Manhattan. Today definitely called for both and it wasn't even noon.

"I don't have a mommy. But my daddy works up there. With my uncle and auntie and my favorite cousin."

Lorelai's gaze followed Ginny's finger out of the window where it landed on the castle. *No way. It couldn't be.*

The only people she knew with that much extended family under that roof was the *royal* family. Which would make Ginny—

"Ginny! Ginny? You're way out of bounds if you're down here. You know—" a deep, booming voice called out from just outside the stable. Ginny froze, as did Lorelai. The child had the good sense to hide behind the stall door, but darn if Lorelai's body didn't betray her at the worst possible moment. Her limbs shut down one by one, the air in the stable thick like water filling her lungs. Drowning her on dry freaking land. Only her heart sped up, pounding against her chest like a war drum.

It was the only thing she could hear, outside the echo of that voice, tumbling around in her head, threatening her sanity.

She *knew* that voice, had tried for a decade to let the masculine timbre roll off her shoulders, stop weighing her down. It was exactly how she remembered it, yet also different. Sexier, stronger, if that was possible. *Well, heck.*

As the owner of the voice rounded the corner, Lorelai's breath halted in her chest. It wasn't only the voice that was sexier, stronger, more masculine. Heck if the past ten years hadn't done Robert, Duke of Puruse, King of Aldonia, a world of good. Wide hands sat atop hips that boasted snug jeans that left little to the imagination.

He squinted, but even in the dull light of the stable, Lorelai saw that his eyes were the same pale blue—maybe the only part of him that was remotely the same. Only the edges showed wear in the thin, almost invisible lines that flanked each eye. Darn men for only getting more good-looking with age. As if she needed another reason to despise him.

He walked toward her and Ginny, rubbing his eyes. Lorelai tried not to stare at the way the striated muscles in his arms pulsed with this simple gesture. He was all muscle, hard edges now. *Christ.*

When she'd known him as a teen, he'd been pudgy, adorable in his know-it-all-ness, but certainly not what one would describe as naturally handsome. Now, though, he could be the model for older men who found the gym late in life, leading to a total transformation.

Oh, goody.

He wasn't only back—the how and why still escaped her for now—but looked better than ever. She had a few choice words brewing for her brother, who hadn't given her so much as a warning. So much for a smooth takeover of the barn and operation. Lorelai's mind was now firmly set on one thing, and one thing only.

She would become the huntsman and make him rue the day he treated her like a child.

"Ginny! You can't be down here, hon. I've already told you this area's off-limits. Horses are dangerous, and you could get hurt." He wrapped his daughter up in his arms, squeezing tightly.

Good gracious, his forearms could move a bus. *Not the time or place to get all doe-eyed again.* Not for a man who still didn't seem to have a clue she inhabited space on this earth.

Instead, she scoffed at his admonition of Ginny, of her "dangerous" animals. Sure, they could be, but only if the rider was cruel or incompetent. If memory served her well, Robert had fallen into the latter category when he was younger, when it came to horses at least. Apparently, not much had changed in that department.

Lorelai muttered as much under her breath. At the sound, Robert looked up, appearing surprised to see her standing there. *So he's as obtuse as ever as well.* Who else did he think would take over after her father passed away?

"Oh, hi. I'm sorry about Ginny. She has a way of sneaking out of the castle that I haven't quite figured out since we got back." He smiled, his teeth bright against the shadows that draped the rest of the stables. She smiled in return, not unkindly, waiting for the more personal greeting she expected from him after so long of not seeing each other. Sure, the attraction had been one-sided, but they were practically family. "So, anyway, I should probably introduce myself. I'm Robert. The King."

What? Her mind registered the polite, benign manner and the utter lack of a clue on his face that he *knew* her. He knew her *well.* Was she really so inconsequential in his life that he couldn't place her familiar face? Because she knew for a fact she hadn't changed that much. She exhaled slowly, bit her tongue until she calmed down.

This brought back a memory Lorelai had pushed to the far recesses of her mind, hadn't recalled in the past ten years. Robert had been out on a date—one of a string of women he went through in college—and this one had crushed Lorelai since the girl was in her eleventh-grade homeroom. He'd walked her down to the stables, pressed her up against the wooden door with such force, the horses had roused. Lorelai had sprinted down the stairs from the apartment above the stables to see what the commotion was, only to witness the intimate moment of Robert's lips fused with her classmate's. At one point, Robert had opened his eyes, his mouth still making quick work of the young woman's, stared directly at Lorelai, smiled out the corner of his mouth, then went about his business.

When she'd seen him heading out the next night and had asked if he was taking that same girl out again, he'd laughed, a humorless bark, and informed her in the haughty tone he'd adopted when he'd begun grooming for his royal heritage that he needed someone older, wiser. At that moment, Lorelai felt her heart split in two.

One part of her, and she wasn't sure which was more dominant, had wanted to leave, become more worldly for him, while the other part of her loathed him. In her youthful lust and inexperience, she recalled with vivid clarity which had won out. A year later and she was headed for America, desperate to make a name for herself. She could tell herself it had nothing to do with her teenage crush, but she'd be lying if every accolade, every award she earned, she didn't picture showing to Robert. To make matters infinitely worse, those were the last years Lorelai would have had with her father—she just hadn't known it then. She didn't blame Robert for that, just herself for being unbearably weak when it came to him. She'd loved him enough to forsake everything else in her life at one point, and it had cost her that—everything.

Now, each cell in her body recalled what it was like to

loathe him, and she was careful to only allow that emotion to surface. Anything else would break her again. She wouldn't survive it a second time, not after what it had taken to rebuild her life. Her*self*.

"I didn't catch your name."

"No, you didn't. I'm busy though, so if you could grab your daughter and let me get back to work, I'd appreciate it." She didn't mean the words to come out as a command, but Jesus, did he have a way of drawing the worst out of her. Just like before, though, she'd use that to drive herself to be better. Stronger without him or the insatiable need she had for his approval.

His attention.

His love.

"Um, sure. You're the new barn manager, right?"

She gave him a polite nod in response but worried if she tried to give a voice to her other thoughts, she would irrevocably crack down the middle for good.

"My brother mentioned something about that when I took the post back here. Well, thanks for keeping an eye out for Ginny. She's always suffered at the hands of a father who doesn't have much of a passion for horses. Maybe you could, um, take her out sometime?"

"Fine," Lorelai spat. "She's welcome any time. Everyone else needs to make an appointment." No matter what blaze his gaze ignited in her, she kept hers pinned to him. She didn't want him thinking he could stop by anytime he wanted. She just couldn't have that. Though she was also well aware it was his birthright to do whatever the hell he wanted around there—that technically, as her boss, he could fire her then and there for insubordination if she didn't get her attitude in check. It was so freaking humiliating that after all this time and growth she was still at the mercy of Robert.

Just one more reason to push for the huntsman position. It would afford her the independence and stature to put some distance between them.

Her eyes broke the lock between them, tears she didn't want him to see threatening behind her lids. She spun around, feeling safer without the scrutiny of his gaze.

His gaze trailed up her spine, leaving a web of shivers as they passed over her. Even now, yet another betrayal stacked against it, her body was aware of him. *Traitor.*

"Do you know who I am?" he asked. She didn't turn around to face him. Couldn't answer while returning the gaze that had grown darker since she'd known him as a boy, loved him from afar. She saw a storm in there, and she had spent long enough in the rain.

"Of course, I do, Your Grace." *But do you know who I am?* She bit back the question on the tip of her tongue, a metallic tinge racing through her mouth, payment for her silence. That was a herculean feat with Robert. *King* Robert. Would she ever get used to that?

She'd known coming home would be difficult, that seeing him again would be like a butter knife slowly and painfully serrating the walls she'd built up over the past ten years, but she thought she'd built them strong. That he'd be nothing but an annoyance. Once again, where he was concerned, she was mistaken.

She hadn't anticipated the liquid heat she'd felt coursing through her when she'd looked up from the sweetest head of curls and was thrown headfirst into his stormy blue-gray eyes that threatened to melt her wall from the inside out.

She didn't like that, not a single, darn bit.

"Well, normally that comes with some sort of respect."

She barked out a laugh devoid of any humor. "Respect is earned. So, earn it."

"And how do I do that?" he said with a growl.

Against everything she stood for, everything she hoped he would see in her, her body betrayed her at that feral, primal sound, weakening her knees and sending a pool of heat and moisture between her legs.

She needed him gone, and fast.

"You start by giving me my space. Ginny is adorable and welcome here whenever she wants to come by, but I'll ask that someone else bring her, *Your Grace*." She hadn't meant that last part to come out as the curse it did, but it was too late now.

"How is my daughter welcome here, and I, the King—the King who owns these stables, might I remind you—am not?" He'd stepped closer to her, Ginny back with Billie Jean and unaware of the drama unfolding around her. With only an arm's length between them now, Lorelai caught the scent of vanilla tobacco and whiskey—one-hundred percent eau de man—and her stomach flipped again. She really wished her body got the memo this man was to be avoided at all costs, no matter how good he smelled, how magnetically sexy he'd become.

"Because she isn't at all like you," she whispered.

"And why, pray tell, isn't she?"

"Well, for starters, she's much too cute, too kind."

"Excuse me, did I offend you in some past life I am not aware of?"

"Something like that," she mumbled, hanging a bridle on the wall beside the stable. "Now, if you can't tell, the stables are a wreck, so I've got a lot to do before dark. You know where the door is."

A pregnant pause hung over the stables as he seemed to measure a response. Lorelai was half convinced he would sack her then and there for her insubordination. He sighed, resigned, though, and the nagging fear unfurled in Lorelai's chest. She was safe. For now.

"Come on, Ginny," he said, his voice soft, hurt.

Tough. It wasn't her problem he'd been so cruel to her in high school, and now added on to the injustice by not recognizing her. He was an adult now, and he could live with the consequences of his choices.

That didn't help her, though, as she saddled up Billie Jean and led her out of the stables. The rogue tears finally fell, heavy and hot as she let the past ten years of disappointment bleed out in the salt water.

As she hit the trail at a gallop, the wind drying the tears as they fell, Lorelai caught a parting image of the man she'd loved her whole life, his daughter's small hand wrapped safely in his as he left her barn, head down in shame. It was going to be harder than she thought, coming home to Aldonia after all the time spent away. As the image shifted to the regal broad shoulders that filled his white dress shirt perfectly, Lorelai shivered.

It would be very hard, indeed.

CHAPTER TWO: THE BOY

He squinted under the piercing midday sun, the heat scorching his skin the way the mystery woman's gaze had branded him. Where had she gone? It had only taken him a matter of minutes to run Ginny up to Aurelia, who'd offered to take her for the afternoon. And then, it had been what, ninety seconds since he'd sprinted down the hill, threw a saddle on the only horse left in the barn, and galloped after the new barn manager who'd all but called him a pompous jerk.

It was the *why* that sat atop his skin, cooling it, even as the sun tried to bake him from the outside in. Why had she been so hell-bent to write him off? From what he'd overheard, Ginny wasn't acting like the terror he'd seen pop up once or twice, mostly when she was hungry or past-tired. The two ladies seemed to be hitting it off, actually.

In fact, seeing the two of them together had done more than ignite his curiosity. The stirrings of something he hadn't felt in quite some time took root in his chest, flowered south. Darn if those two didn't seem like natural partners in crime, and darn if that wasn't all he'd wanted for Ginny. The mother his arrogance had cost his daughter.

But none of what had transpired in his recent past explained the ice wafting off the new woman where he was concerned.

He'd been a helluva better leader since his brother, Philip, had met Aurelia, tightened the sails of the royal ship they'd been steering into the rocks. That was almost four years ago now, so if she was holding on to his policies from before that, taking them personally, then to hell with her.

Except he couldn't write her off the same way she'd done to him. There was an unmistakable familiarity about the barn manager he couldn't place. He knew her, though.

He swore he knew her.

He plied his heels into the horse's ribs and pulled the reins forward. Robert lurched as the stallion raced toward a small opening in the trees.

Jesus. This guy put every other horse to shame. He tucked his body against the strong neck, pulled his knees in against the solid frame, and let the horse guide him through the low-hanging boughs, over the exposed and gnarled roots. There wasn't a chance to appreciate the majesty of the terrain they covered, but it wasn't lost on Robert how little of his country he'd seen firsthand.

Later. There's time for that later. Now, he and the horse were partners on a less-than-stealthy mission, crashing through the underbrush in an attempt to chase down the barn manager. Without warning, the horse slowed to a trot, throwing Robert shoulder-first against the now-rigid neck of the horse.

He growled at the pain that shot down his arm and spread numbness back up. It had to happen to his bad shoulder, too. When they'd slowed to a stop, Robert glanced up, and what remained of his breath was expelled in a gasp as he took in his surroundings. To heck with his shoulder.

A brook bubbled in front of him, meandering between

the lime-green ferns and berry bushes they'd been traipsing through. A sandy outcropping was just across the way, a perfect place to sit and have a picnic, if he could ever find his way back there again. Had the horse not stopped, he doubted he ever would have noticed the pale-blue ribbon snaking its way through his land. He inhaled the scent of his childhood spent outdoors, though how he'd missed this place he couldn't figure out. How much didn't he know about the place he'd been raised, the place he'd ruled for nearly a decade?

More than he'd like to admit, most likely. It wasn't a secret that he'd been aloof before Ginny had been born, and since then had doggedly tried to be the best father and King he could be. It didn't exactly leave much time for meandering throughout his countryside, though. Something he regretted at that moment.

"Hey there, buddy. Why'd we stop?" he asked, patting the horse on the shoulder while he gained his bearings. The sun fell in sheets, pierced by the trees. It had to be ten degrees cooler under the dense canopy. The horse—still a nameless beast who'd stranded him in the middle of nowhere—just snorted and drank greedily from the stream. Robert slid easily off his saddle and in the same motion, grabbed the reins, securing them to the nearest maple. He felt a weight slide off him at the same time, barely perceptible, but he felt lighter nonetheless.

"What the hell are you doing?"

A chill trickled over Robert's skin as the sharp words pierced his usually tough exterior. His groin ached at the thickness of the mystery woman's timbre, betraying him yet again where she was concerned. He looked up, understanding why they'd landed at that particular spot. The barn manager trotted in on her mare, who paused beside him, joining his horse in a water break. This must be why his horse had known where to go; it was probably their watering hole away from the barn.

Robert took a break from admiring the creek and

foliage to appreciate the way the deep-V of the barn manager's t-shirt exposed the top of tanned, ample breasts. He gave a silent prayer of thanks each time her mare shimmied along the shoreline in search of a better angle, heaving the woman's breasts up and down in a motion that would have hypnotized Robert if she hadn't coughed, shook him out of his ardent admiration of her body.

"Tying up." He hid a grin as he slipped the rope a final time through itself, shortening the lead. He might have been inappropriate as hell, but dang if he didn't get some small sense of satisfaction at making her as uncomfortable as she'd made him in his own barn.

She grunted out a curse he didn't quite catch as she jumped off her horse—while it was still moving—and strode over to him, hands on her hips. God, how he wished he was those hands, cupping her curvy figure. If he was lucky enough to start at those ample hips, though, he wouldn't be able to stop there. Every inch of this woman was like a live wire that zapped him, woke him up, and turned him on. He was well aware she could electrocute him if he wasn't careful, though.

"You're doing it wrong," she scolded. She tied off her horse, then walked over to his knot, examining it. He leaned back against the tree, folded his arms over his chest, and watched as she scrutinized his work. There was no way she'd find a fault with his work. At least he could be confident in that.

"I'm not," he told her, biting back a laugh at her frustration. "You roped off like an American. Where are you from?"

She eyed him suspiciously, ignored his question. *So not from there.* One point to him in getting closer to solving the mystery. "How'd you get here so fast?" At least she left his knot alone, seeming to find it acceptable, if not to her liking.

"Don't ask me. Ask Geronimo, here. He's lightning through the woods." If she thought he'd forget to keep coming back to his unanswered questions, she had another thing coming. She didn't seem to have much patience for him, but he could do this all day long with her. The thought of a sparring match with her made him half-hard beneath his already-snug jeans.

"Should be—he was raised on these trails."

"Well, he did his job. Got me to you." He looked up, let his smile reach her, and couldn't help but notice the heat that crept up her chest and spread to her neck and cheeks. Well, dang, that was a reaction more acceptable than her contempt. He crossed his legs, hoping to hide his more-than-obvious attraction to her.

"You shouldn't have taken him out."

"They're my horses; I'll do as I please."

"They're not your horses, you arrogant jerk. And this one needed a new shoe. That's why Dexter didn't come along."

"Dexter, huh? Well, he'll be fine. I'll shoe him myself when we get back."

"Since when do you know how to shoe a horse? I'll handle it. You'll just screw it up." The certainty laced in her voice had him reeling. She knew him, too, and she seemed to figure out from where before him. Why did he feel that was a fatal error on his part?

This whole scene was frustrating as hell. Normally, he was damn good with names and faces—a necessary part of his job—but with her, he couldn't place either, only a vague familiarity and roaring attraction.

The woman bent down to inspect Dexter's right foot, avoiding his gaze expertly. *Eff that.* He was damn good with horses—had been since he'd come back from college and had to take the early crown. His heart pulled at the memory of being forced to learn from the stable hand rather than his own father, one of a million things the man would never be able to teach him after his plane went down on a routine flight to the Republic of Georgia.

God, he missed his father.

Robert shook the cobwebs of memories of his father from his head and bent down to help. It was his horse, his responsibility. So, why was she so hell-bent on fixing it?

He didn't expect the jolt of electricity when his skin grazed hers. Nor how welcome the touch was as the electric tremors abated.

Soft. She was so soft. He'd been expecting her skin to be as tough as the rest of her exterior, but it felt like running his hand over satin.

He also wasn't expecting to meet her gaze, only to find tears building along the lids of her eyes, causing them to shimmer in the speckled light. She was sad, almost like she could read his mind and feel the weight of memory, of loss as he could.

He was mesmerized, captivated by her complexity until she tore her hand from his and shoved his chest, toppling him on his ass to the damp, spongy earth.

Well, heck. Complex was an understatement.

"Don't ever touch me again. *Ever.* Do you hear me?" Her voice rang out over the small meadow, and he didn't have a doubt that everyone within a square mile heard her. Forget the half-hard-on, he was at full-mast now. Though she'd pushed him, all but spat on his face, he was turned on as hell. *Christ, why can't I stop falling for women who want nothing to do with me?*

"You lost the chance to touch me a long time ago." That last sentence he almost didn't catch. Like the surprise at finding her skin soft to the touch, it completely disarmed him to hear her voice as a breath on the wind, barely audible. That didn't even take into account her words. Her damning words. *I lost the chance to touch her. When?* God, how he wished he could go back to that precise moment—whenever it had been—and take this woman in his arms, earn her trust.

Instead, he shot up, devoted to the idea of making that happen now. What could he lose?

He wheeled on her, placed his hands on her shoulders,

pressed her against the tree he'd tied Dexter to, careful to not hurt her. Still, her skin singed his hands where her shoulders were exposed, and he wondered if she felt it, too. The red blush emanating from his fingers up her neck again told him he wasn't alone in his wanting.

She trembled beneath him, her gaze pulled to the water. He wanted her eyes on him, only him.

"You know, raising a hand to the King is a crime against the crown. You could go to prison. Or worse."

"Please," she spat. "You wouldn't dare. You were always spoiled, but never stupid."

Always? How do I know her? More importantly, how does she know me?

"True. But that's not me now, you're right. You won't lay a hand on me, not really." Though as the words left his mouth, open and poised, he imagined her laying her lips on him. Touching them to skin. Caressing. He imagined they would be rough, but tender, much like the rest of her. And hell if it wasn't all he could think about, then.

"How would you know what I would or would not do?" She pressed her face as close to his as she could without touching it. He need only move an inch and his mouth could be on hers, claiming it, silencing the vitriol she spat at him every chance she got. Lord knew he'd wanted nothing else since he'd walked in and seen the siren talking, no *playing with* his daughter, teaching her while she fueled Ginny's imagination.

"Because you would have by now. It's no secret you despise me, but what I can't figure out is why. I'm sorry for that—you have no idea how much I wish I could place where I know you. How much I wish I could go back and make it right so you wouldn't look at me like you are right now."

He brushed the pad of his thumb along her chin where a lone tear had spilled over. He'd hurt her. Maybe not the version of himself that stood before her now, but at some point, he'd hurt her, and he hated himself for it.

"You're different. Maybe you've changed so much you forgot I ever existed. I always knew you didn't pay much attention to me—not like I did you. But to not recognize me? It's cruel, Robert."

His name on her lips was too much for him to bear. He closed the inches between them, covered her quivering bottom lip with his mouth, pulling it into his. He sucked on it until she opened for him, inviting him to explore with small, tentative sweeps of her tongue.

Oh, Christ. She tasted like cinnamon, like just-out-of-the-oven apple pie, warm and wet. He was a goner. When she exhaled, her breath hot on his lips, a soft purr coming from her throat, he knew he was royally screwed. He didn't even know her name, and she'd branded him, claimed him as her own. He didn't care, not as long as she kept running her tongue along his bottom lip. As long as she continued that breathy sigh that made him weak in the joints, hard in other places.

He ran his fingers along her ponytail, loosing the tie in the back, sending her curls tumbling over her shoulders. Her auburn hair was thick as the woods they were in, and now his hands were lost in it, desperate to stay hidden in her forever. He pulled her head closer to his, drawing her body up against his. Her chest rose and fell in quick succession, each exhale a moan of pleasure, driving him mad with desire.

He thought he'd known passion before, had known pleasure, but it was nothing compared to this moment with the mystery woman whose tongue tangled with his, whose breath was a part of him now, searing him from the inside out.

As quickly as he'd pounced on her, she pulled away, her bottom lip swollen and wet with him. Her chest rose and fell, her hair now delicately draped over her breasts. If she was at all intoxicating to him thirty minutes ago, that was nothing compared to the way she'd wormed her way into his body, his life now.

And he didn't even know her name.

"Please. Tell me who you are," he begged. He placed a tender kiss atop her forehead, felt the shimmer of sweat from their exertion. He licked his lips, tasting her, finding that along with the salt, there was a hint of vanilla.

"I have to go." Her breath was hot on his chest, so when she backed away from him, he felt the loss keenly, his skin like ice where she'd warmed him then left him exposed. In a flash, she'd undone her horse's tie and was up in the saddle. In less time, she was riding away from him as fast as he'd ridden in after her.

Not on his life was he letting her get away with continuing to run from him. He'd pull rank if he had to, but only as a last resort. He wanted this woman, wanted her to want him in return, but not because of who he was. He'd been there before and the only good thing to come of that was Ginny.

In less than thirty seconds, he was tearing after her, the ride into the grove nothing compared to the way he and Dexter cornered the trees, dodged the branches that jabbed at them like jousters vying for his crown. All he thought as the wind snaked through his hair, danced down his shirt where her chest had been pressed just moments before, was that this woman had come into his life for a reason, and after that searing kiss, he had an idea what that might be.

Only moments later, the barn was in sight and she dismounted just seconds before he got to her. A man came out to greet her, wrapped her up in an embrace, and kissed her cheek. She hugged him back tightly, and so help him, Robert wanted to pummel the guy.

Then his insides turned to ice as he thought about what that meant. What he'd just done. *No. Oh, Jesus, no.* Had he just kissed a married woman? His track record was crap when it came to that, but nothing about her signaled a significant other in the picture. Yet, had he thought to look for the most obvious evidence—a ring? Even now, he couldn't picture anything other than her lips parted for him, a sheen of his moisture causing them to sparkle in the sun. Damn. What was he thinking? As he rode his horse full speed up to the barn door, there was no mistaking the smile on the man's face as he lifted her, twirled her around.

When the man stopped and released her, and Robert had dismounted, he saw that the guy with the barn manager was Gregory, his younger brother's best friend and member of the royal guard. *No effing way.* Since his track record included sleeping with his brother's fiancé, he didn't think it would go over even remotely okay if he'd kissed Gregory's wife—even though he didn't know she was married. Somehow, that would only make it worse, especially since he didn't even know her name. God, he was every bit the ass she'd decided he was, wasn't he?

As if she'd read his mind, the woman saw Robert coming and tucked her head to her chest, picked up her pace into the stables. He'd fix that wrong later. Better to start with the bigger issue—the jilted spouse, his staff member. But when Gregory followed her, Robert sighed. It looked like he'd be tackling two apologies for the pain of one. It was imperative he set the record straight.

She'd done nothing wrong. It had been him who'd ardently pursued her, even after she'd asked him to leave her alone. To stop touching her. Even though that was the last thing he wanted to do; even now, in the face of an entirely new set of circumstances, he wanted her with a ferocity that scared him.

Halfway down the length of the barn, Gregory stopped in his tracks and wheeled on Robert. Robert braced himself for the inevitable blow, but nothing came. Instead, he was greeted with a smile, an extended hand.

"Your Grace."

"If you don't start calling me Robert outside of formal events, I'm going to have you thrown in the lake."

Gregory laughed, shook Robert's hand with gusto. It only made Robert feel worse for the news he had to share.

His crime. Not hers. A crime he would commit again if given the chance. Maybe that was why he felt a heaviness in his shoulders, a churning in his gut. He didn't feel half as guilty as he should.

"Fine. But what, pray tell, did you two fight about this time? I swear she was always getting flustered over you, and not always in a good way. Now she barely said hi to me. She's been gone a decade and all I get is a hug? Heck no." Gregory laughed, but Robert was stunned silent.

No. Not possible. Was it her? No. It couldn't be. But… But she'd had glasses, not to mention short, mousy hair back then. A stick-thin body with the flattest chest Robert had seen on a girl in high school. Still, now that he thought about it…

Now that Gregory said it, he wondered how he missed the sharp line of her jaw, the espresso eyes that saw into an animal's soul. They were Lebedev eyes, but her gaze—one that threatened to undo him with its passion, its fury—was all her own.

"Um, well, she met Ginny." He fell over himself, trying to find words that didn't seem like they were strung together by his four-year-old daughter. "And then she took her horse out. I followed her."

"Yeah, I see that. You okay, sire?"

Robert didn't know what to say to that as he watched her rub down the rough edges of Dexter's bare hoof. Was he? Would he ever be okay again now that she was back in his life and held him accountable for the schmuck he was when he was younger?

"Well, thanks for welcoming Lorelai home. I know she's happy to see you, whether or not she's being a good host right now. Hey, on another note, is Ginny up there? I found some of those newts she was chasing last week and thought I'd take her to see them."

Robert nodded, struck mute.

"Cool. Well, tell that girl over there I'll see her tonight. Family dinner at seven, right?"

Robert could only nod. Gregory patted him on the back and with the light pressure, he could have fallen backward had a post not been there to steady him. When he thought back to Lorelai's anger, her words laced with resentment, he had no doubt he'd misread the situation.

Fatally misread it.

Because the only thing that would get him in more trouble than falling for Gregory's wife was falling for his sister. His baby sister who had pined after Robert her whole childhood. He'd been a jerk back then, insensitive and arrogant, but his parents' deaths had knocked that out of him. He'd been forced home, shoved into a royal life that didn't include any of the partying or skirt-chasing he'd grown used to. He'd become a king in the making.

She hadn't witnessed any of that, though. She'd loved the fool, and now he had to live with the consequences of that.

Suddenly, Robert was seventeen again, about to head to university, a young girl four years his junior chasing his car down the road. Ten years may have passed, but he couldn't shake the feeling that she wasn't done putting him in his place, and that he deserved everything coming his way.

It would be a hell of a summer. Though he knew it would come back to bite him where it would hurt most, he wasn't as resentful of having to work in the south castle this summer while renovations to the capitol were completed. No, as he recalled Lorelai's very unflat breasts pressed up against his chest, her luminous, wavy hair cascading across her taut back, he thought no matter what sins he had to repent for, he wouldn't mind being home again.

Maybe he'd drum up a few new transgressions while he was there. Make the repenting worth it. He whistled as he made his way down the stalls to Lorelai, desperate to reintroduce himself. He had a lot to make up for, and he wanted to start right away.

CHAPTER THREE: THE BEGINNING

She felt his presence before his hand rested on her shoulder. He was iron, she a magnet—him hard as steel and causing her to pulse with a physical need to be near him. She hated her body for giving in to its desires over what would certainly be the more prudent choice.

The shock to her system at his touch sent currents of heat down her stomach, chills back up her spine. It took every ounce of her waning self-control to not wheel around and face him. She knew exactly what would happen if she did, and it didn't serve a single one of her interests to finish the kiss they'd started a week ago.

As soon as the thought was formed, though, her body reacted viscerally to the idea of one particular interest that might be served by Robert. One that had been woefully unattended to for longer than she cared to admit.

You'd so better not be the harpy that gives up her self-esteem for a quick lay.

That self-admonition didn't do anything to shut up the part of her that was acting like a horny teenager. All she could come up with was that Robert was the hottest man she'd ever laid eyes on before she gave up and turned to face him.

"I've been looking for you all week. Why won't you answer my calls?"

Because I'm still not over you. Their kiss her first full day back had shown her what she'd already known—that she would never fully be able to love anyone the way she loved Robert, which was a tragedy of epic proportions considering she also knew there wasn't any future in that one-sided longing, especially not since he was crowned King. What was once an age-appropriate crush had turned cancerous, consuming her and all but killing any desire she had for anyone but him. If she had any sense, she'd run from this job, from her childhood, from her past, and straight into one of the many proposals she'd received in New York. Romantic and otherwise.

At least she'd done the impossible and against her better judgment said yes to a date with Simon, the huntsman that evening. That was a step in the right direction that had two unforeseen benefits—it lit the path away from Robert and the hold he had over her, and it allowed her to talk to the current huntsman before she made a play for his job. Though at that moment, she couldn't imagine opening her door to anyone but the man who was in front of her.

Robert. With his tight t-shirt that looked like a second skin it was so snug. She had the sense he was carved from stone—solid and cool—if she hadn't been pressed up against his fleshy heat just a few days ago.

"I was cubbing up at the mountain fixture with the staff so we could make sure everything goes well for your hunt next month." That was only partially true. They'd gotten back two nights prior, and while she could blame what the riders called a "hunting hangover" for her reticence to come down the day before, the hard truth was she wasn't sure she wanted to see Robert yet. Or ever.

"Bull."

Seriously? He was calling her out?

"You were avoiding me."

"I don't have anything to say to you. I sent the purchase order to you for the feed and shavings. That's all for this month. Just email me if there's a problem." She kept working, mucking the stall in front of her so it shined like it had never housed Billie Jean. Anything to duck the eyes that looked like another storm brewing. A trickle of sweat raced down her spine, proof of her diligence in avoiding the man behind her.

"I already approved it. You'll have it by the end of the week."

"Thanks," she muttered, her heart breaking at the benign conversation. Why wouldn't he leave her alone? He didn't go down to the staff housing and check in on them. *He probably didn't go around kissing them, either.*

"Lorelai, look at me."

She sighed, resigned, and turned slowly to face him. Her gaze was stuck between his chest—impossibly broad and strong—and his eyes, dangerously blue like an icy pond that would claim her life if she spent too long in their depths. Why couldn't he have gotten fat, gone bald? The term *dad bod* had to have come from somewhere, but Robert's photo wouldn't be under that entry in the dictionary. Not with his solid oak chest, arms that looked strong enough to lift a horse, and that chiseled jaw she'd held fast to just days before.

No, Robert was sexy as hell and that wasn't doing her any favors.

"I didn't know. I was so stupid, so blind. How didn't I see you in there?" His hand had migrated to her hip, his thumb pressed against the spot where her thigh met her abdomen. It was everything she'd waited so long to hear, to feel, but he was too late. Maybe if he'd had any inkling who she was when he'd wandered down to the barn to retrieve his daughter, she'd feel differently, but that wasn't the case. Not even close. Per usual, he hadn't seen her.

"Maybe because you didn't want to admit you treated me like dirt when we were kids."

He sighed, his breath warm on the top of her head. It made her dizzy. "I'm sorry. You have to know that wasn't me. Well, it was, but it hasn't been for quite some time."

"And you think that excuses you?"

"I don't."

"So, then what's your point?" She didn't want to be pissed, couldn't handle the guilt when he looked at her like he was the injured one. But then she'd recall him pressed against the wall of her father's barn with a girl he had no intention of seeing again juxtaposed against her pressed against a tree when he didn't even know her name, and rage would rise up like bile.

"My point is I'm sorry. I'd like to start over. Maybe take my horses out for a ride and talk. Just talk."

She was pretty sure he added the last part when her cheeks flushed with heat at the idea of going back out for a ride with him. He wouldn't be wrong in thinking her mind had wandered to dangerous territory, but it was brought back as soon as she registered his casual mention of "his horses." Her libido subsided, and anger brewed in its place.

"They're not yours." *Crap.* Had she said that out loud?

"What aren't?"

Crap, crap, crap. He'd heard her.

"The horses. My father's stables. He built them, cared for them, loved each animal who came through here like it was his own. Just because they're on your land doesn't mean you have any claim to them."

He smiled. Actually smiled, and her anger turned to rage. If she could get her hands on him, she had no doubt she'd ignite him in the flames that engulfed her.

"Actually, that's exactly what it means."

"You think that because you purchased the land with money you yourself didn't earn, that because your family paid for its construction, that it belongs to you, but that isn't true. It takes showing up, putting in the work, the sweat, the back-breaking time. It takes being there in the middle of the night when a foal is sick to feed her, to curl up beside her so she doesn't freeze with fever. You might call them yours on paper, but they're my birthright by other counts."

He seemed to consider that, drawing his brows closer, his gaze sharp but unreadable. She wanted to be smug, righteous in her argument that seemed not to have a rebuttal. That was until he looked at her with a glimmer in his eye she recalled from when they were kids. He was up to no good and she'd probably be on the receiving end of it. *Dang it.*

His arms crossed over his chest, he nodded, so shallow a gesture that she barely caught it.

"Okay."

She shot him a look that demanded more, but he either didn't see it or pretended not to. God, he was infuriating.

"Okay? What's that supposed to mean?"

"It means okay. You're right. They're yours."

"Don't be cryptic, Robert." It was strangely satisfying but also horribly out of place to use his name, but she'd be buggered if she recognized his title with the honorific if he wouldn't give her the respect she deserved. He hadn't known who she was when he'd kissed her, and now he expected that just because he apologized she was supposed to consider it all behind them? No. Absolutely not. "Explain what the Sam Hell you mean and then let me get back to my job."

"I mean the stables are yours. I'll sign them over to you today."

She stopped where she was and tried with every cell in her body to talk her lungs into resuming their sole duty.

Breathe.

In.

Out.

But her breath halted in her chest and refused to start

back up again. Surely he didn't mean what she thought she'd heard. She turned from him, afraid the heat building up behind her eyes would spill over, make a fool of her more than Robert already had.

"You'd give me the stables? Just like that?" she asked. She hated that her voice broke when she realized how much hope was laced in her question. She'd come back for that reason and that reason only, but she thought it would be harder to get. That she'd have to earn it. And she was prepared for that. This, though? The simple handing over of the dream she'd clung to when her father passed away? It was too much.

"Not just the stables. The horses, the staff, all of it. Of course, the operating budget will still run out of the castle since we use the horses and hounds for the hunts and all that. Is that acceptable?"

Is that acceptable? Is he kidding? She turned back to face him, hoping to find some clue as to whether he would be cruel enough to tease her with an offer that would, quite literally, change her life, give her everything she'd ever wanted. Well, almost.

Instead, a smile graced his lips, his eyes bright, unwavering from hers.

He is serious.

Lorelai thought of her father, how proud he would be of her, how much he'd wanted this life for her and Gregory. It was why he'd stayed at the royal stables after his wife passed away giving birth to her.

"It is. It's more than just acceptable, Robert." She braced her arms against Billie Jean's stable door, and the mare licked her bare skin affectionately. Her instinct was to reach for Robert, embrace him for his thoughtfulness, but she couldn't relinquish the tiny shred of self-control she'd gained over the last week where he was concerned. Not just yet. "But why?"

"Because you're right. These should have been in your family for two decades already. I'm sorry it's taken this long for me to see that. I've been negligent in more than one way, it seems."

"What about Gregory?" She didn't want to take the birthright away from her brother, but knew he'd long since lost the love for the horses when he'd lost their father. That was the sole connection Gregory had to her and her father's work. With him gone and Lorelai in New York, unable to keep the stables going, that tenuous bond was severed. She only hoped that she would be able to repair it now that she was back. Gregory was all she had left.

"I've already seen to it that he has land in his name— that all Dukes in the royal guard have land that will be deeded to future heirs and stay in their family name forever. These are yours, Lorelai."

The heat stinging her eyes manifested in large, hot tears streaming down her face. She wished she'd worn waterproof mascara, but then, she'd had no idea her life would change in the matter of a moment when she'd headed down from the apartment that morning. Half of her wanted to kiss him while the other half wanted to wallop him for such an unceremonious gesture.

"Thank you, Robert. It's the kindest thing anyone has ever done for me."

She sniffed and wiped the moisture from between her nose and upper lip. Why couldn't she be at least a moderately attractive crier? She knew her eyes were swollen, damp, and her nose cherry red. And he was still devastatingly handsome. *Ugh.*

"Of course. It was already yours because it was your father's." He coughed, skirted her glance for a moment. "Would, uh, would you like to have dinner tonight to talk about the details? I can swing by and walk with you to the castle. Patricia has been making American dishes for Aurelia all week. Apparently she's been craving only comfort foods with this baby."

Lorelai paused before she answered. The tears still came, but with burning frustration now that she understood the intention behind his offer. It wasn't noble at all. He wanted to get in her pants and had the funds to make sure she was well-paid for the effort. He was still a dog, albeit in George Clooney's skin with an impeccable wardrobe.

"Dinner tonight?"

"Yes," he said, moving toward her, drawing a finger down her arm, eliciting goosebumps on her skin. It made her feel dirty, not at all what she was sure he intended. "We could eat on my private terrace, go over the details of the transfer of ownership. Plus, it will be nice to get to know you again. All grown up."

Robert grinned, his crooked smile weakening her resolve to tell him to go to hell. She fought off the urge to place her lips where a muscle ticked in his jaw, to kiss the spot tenderly. It took all of her fortitude to see through his words, his scent, to the purpose behind his more than generous offer.

He thought he'd laid a foolproof trap, but he didn't take one thing into consideration—she *had* grown up while she was away, and apparently he was using the same tired tricks to lure women into his bed.

Well, not her. Not this time.

"What an interesting proposition. You, me, alone after all this time." Her voice dripped with feigned sensuality, mire bubbling just below the surface. That, he missed entirely, as evidenced by the way he leaned closer into her, the heady musk emanating off him in waves, testing her resolve. His fatal flaw wouldn't be hers.

"I'll have wine brought up from the cellar. I'm so looking forward to this, Lory."

And there it was, the nickname he'd used when she was a gangly, nerdy thing, her one-sided romance all that drove her. It was always a swift dismissal of her then, and it remained the same now. The quick, clipped way he'd used it brought her fully back to the man who'd broken her heart all those years ago. He was still in there, still the selfish prince, even if his title had changed.

"Well, you enjoy that. I've got a date, but I'll be around this week when you get those details drawn up," she said, tossing her hair over her shoulder and turning abruptly from him. "Oh, and I'll insist on paying you for the property. Please have it in writing that I will give you full market value for the operation, to be paid with my monthly salary. When I earn the title of huntswoman, I'll be able to pay you more."

"A date?" Was she mistaken or had his voice become shrill?

She threw a glance over her shoulder and tried not to relish in the confusion building in his sharp features.

She barely suppressed a grin when he bit the corner of his lip, rubbed his furrowed brow. It was fine with her if he didn't acknowledge the latter part of her little speech. There would be time for that. For now, she'd put him in his place. The fact that he backed up from where he was standing and landed his perfectly shined loafers in manure was just icing on a cake that was perfectly sweet already. She'd get the horses, the stables, and the property, and could still work her way to huntsman. The first female huntsman in Aldonia. All in a good day's work.

Before she turned back around to him, she plastered her best aren't-I-the-sweetest-thing-since-ice-cream smile on her face.

"Yep. He's actually showing up in the next few minutes, so I'd better head up to my apartment and get ready. It's not often a stable gal gets to put on a tiny dress and hit the dance floor."

"A date." His voice had regained its regal control, but it hadn't lost the incredulity.

Wow. He was slower than she remembered. Not that she minded having the upper hand. She didn't, not one bit.

She nodded, swallowing a giggle.

"Yep. A real, honest-to-goodness date."

When his gaze trailed over her, she felt it like the bridge

of his hand followed his eyes. She hoped he was imagining the tiny dress she'd slipped into conversation with the sole intention of riling him up.

"With whom? I didn't know you had a boyfriend."

"I don't. He's a new interest. And you didn't know my name a week ago, so consider it a possibility that you don't know all there is to know about me anymore, *Bobby*."

Out of the corner of her eye as she gathered the new gelding's tack to bring over to the washroom, she caught the drop of his jaw, the steely look of a king. *Good*. She'd used the nickname on purpose, knowing from her brother's needling of the man when he was younger that it was certain to piss him right off. Just as his nickname for her had done. *Tit for tat*.

"Was what I did to you back then really so unforgivable?" he pleaded. She heard his voice crack and almost turned back around at the hurt in his voice. *Almost*.

"No, but being forgiven doesn't mean I have to go back to how things were when I was fifteen, either. I understand if that means the deal is off."

She fought every urge in her body to turn around when he sighed, as a defeated sound as she'd ever heard come from a man, especially this man.

"I'm not so big a jerk that I would offer something like that and just take it back."

Okay, she wanted to tell him. *Prove it*.

"I'll send you the paperwork by the end of this week with the payment schedule you requested. You might want a lawyer to go over it with you, so I'll have Nico drop it off."

"I've got my own lawyer, but thank you. It really is a generous offer, and I really am grateful." All of which was true, so why did she feel her stomach drop out from under her as she spoke the words?

Because they were only half of what she wanted to say, wanted to do.

It was the thoughts she swallowed into the cavity below

her heart that ate away at her. She wanted to tell him thank you, not just for the offer, which made her eyes well up with tears at the generosity, but for the kiss. For making at least the fifteen-year-old Lorelai happy, even if it was at the expense of her grown self. Because the honest truth was that she'd never be over him.

She'd spent years pining for a man she knew as intimately as she could from afar, and he didn't even recognize her when she'd returned home. It was too cruel, the obvious irony in her longing. The last part of her silence was an ache deep in her stomach, and lower, filled with renewed longing. Stronger than what had sustained her through crappy dates in New York or sent her to bed above the barn her senior year touching herself because the man she wished would do the job was busy with someone else on the floor below.

This was the longing, the lust of a woman who'd learned how to feel, to ache for love, to wish for it on the darkest nights, and work through the lack of it on the longest days. It had matured, as she had, which was why she knew she would never be free of it.

"Well, then I'll be seeing you. Have a good night."

His footsteps receded, softly disappearing as if he'd never been there. But the chill that shot up her spine as she finally freed her feet from the ground to force herself to get ready for another date she didn't want to be on told another story. He'd been there, all right, and all she wanted at that moment was for him to come strolling back, to wrap her in his arms, and finish the kiss they'd begun a week ago.

Knowing that wasn't in her future, certainly not in her night to come, she sighed, brushed a rogue tear from her cheek, and went in search of a little black dress that might make her feel remotely better for telling the one man she'd ever loved to screw off.

CHAPTER FOUR: THE PROGRESS

Robert pulled the curtains back as far as he could without giving away his position. He'd shut off the light so as to avoid being backlit like some horror movie lothario, but damn if he didn't feel every bit the part.

The huntsman's car had pulled up half an hour ago and it was still there. Why the heck was he still parked in her driveway? Robert swallowed back images of what else might still be parked over there, feeling them clanging around in his stomach.

He sighed, pushed back off the window, and retreated to the bar in his suite. After pouring himself three fingers of scotch, he paced six laps before giving up and resuming his vigil.

Still there. Still hidden from view. Jesus, what the hell were they up to? She had to work tomorrow. Memories of similar late nights Robert had spent in the barn came unbidden, the myriad of faces he'd pressed his against taunting him now with sneers of exactly what Lorelai was probably up to.

He took a long pull of his drink, the heat warming him from the center out. All it did was ignite the flames that lapped at his heart and mind, threatening an inferno.

Where had this obsession with Lorelai come from? He admitted that when she'd lived there, he'd barely known who she was outside his younger brother's best friend's sister, the stable manager's daughter. Even when she'd left for New York, and the decade that passed until she returned, not once had she crossed his mind. And why should she have? She was eighteen when she left, barely a woman.

But now? *Oh, God.*

Now she was back, all curves and soft valleys for him to explore, and he couldn't keep his mind on anything else. Nothing had been simple since she'd walked back into his life. Heck, he'd even burned his microwave popcorn the night before because he'd been too wrapped up in thoughts of how to make his lifetime of neglect up to her, that he hadn't registered the kernels had stopped popping and started roasting. The acrid, smoky scent still lingered in the air as a reminder of his stupidity.

He was a first-rate fool, and aware of that, but short of rigging up a machine to shoot him back fifteen years to start over with her, he wasn't quite sure what to do.

Hence the stalker tendencies he'd developed.

Movement caught his eye, and he darted back behind the curtain, one eye discreetly keeping watch on the happenings below.

He recognized Lorelai immediately, or rather his groin did, roaring to life when he caught sight of the minuscule dress—*if one could even call it that*—she wore. The fabric clung tight to her hips, hips he recalled in his hands as if they were there now. Hips that had branded him, claimed him.

Worse was the fact that someone else's hands were on them now. As she walked him down the path to his car, a proprietary arm draped her waist, an arm Robert envisioned breaking in two if the huntsman moved it any further south than it already was.

Halfway there, they stopped, and the huntsman leaned

down to Lorelai. Curse the angle. Robert wanted to see her face, see if she was happy or not. His brain argued that she could take care of herself, but the parts of him that were less than critical added he might as well make sure.

That was how he found himself in front of the barn less than thirty seconds later, out of breath despite the fact he'd been running three miles around the property each morning. He crept along the courtyard of the barn until the huntsman's car came into view. Robert peeked his head around the oak slats, trying in earnest to catch his breath.

Again, he was met with a crappy angle. All he could see was the huntsman crouched over Lorelai, one hand on her waist, the other on the car above her shoulder. A hurricane of emotion roiled in his chest, one part protectiveness over Lorelai, the other rampant jealousy of the huntsman. He knew the man had a name—he'd been hired on that and the reputation it preceded alone—but he refused to use it when the schmuck was pouncing on the lips Robert craved, that had singed Robert's with their heat.

The idea that the heat could be placed elsewhere had Robert pacing behind the barn, muttering to himself. This wasn't how a king behaved, but he could no sooner talk himself off the ledge than he could storm up to Lorelai and her date and intervene with a swift jab to the man's jugular.

Even if he did wonder if Lorelai felt trapped, unable to walk away. *Hmmm.* Maybe he should check in and at least make sure Lorelai was safe.

So he did what any self-respecting man would do. He walked up to the couple, who he could see now were only talking. Had that been the case the whole time, or had they just taken a break from necking to come up for air? Robert coughed, his eyes trained on the huntsman.

The man didn't surprise easy, that was for certain. He simply glanced up, languid eyes giving Robert a once-over before turning his attention back to Lorelai. In different circumstances, and if Robert were a better man, he'd have understood, but neither applied.

Lorelai, however, after recovering from the shock of seeing Robert there in the middle of the night, pulled out from under the huntsman's arm and put distance between them. Robert watched as she straightened her dress, tugging it down before realizing that the gesture exposed her perfect, voluptuous breasts even more.

It was a win-win for Robert, who enjoyed either way the argument went.

He bit down on his bottom lip to suppress a smile that only disappeared when he saw the same appraising gaze he gave Lorelai on the huntsman's face. If he wasn't King…

"Your Grace," the huntsman said, dipping his head, but not moving his body an inch—definitely a break in royal protocol that was made on purpose. Oh, well, Robert would handle that another day. Now he just wanted the man to slink back to where he'd come from and leave Lorelai with Robert.

"You can leave, Simon," Robert replied, his gaze still glued to Lorelai as she made one last and fruitless, attempt to cover herself in the amount of fabric Ginny used to dress her dolls. But God, did he like watching Lorelai try. Her dress left little to the imagination, and Robert's pants tightened around the zipper thanks to a half-mast erection.

What he wouldn't give to slide the fabric down her curves, leave it in a pile at their feet, then pay special attention to each inch that had been hidden beneath the dress.

Simon gave another curt nod and bent down to plant two kisses on Lorelai's cheeks, a little too close to her mouth for Robert to feel it was a chaste gesture, but at least the infernal man was leaving.

At that moment, he wished he'd hired the other huntsman from Albania, a round, chubby man who just also happened to be lightning in the saddle. But, no, Robert had worried over what a portly man might say about the way Robert ran the country, especially since huntsmen were notorious lotharios and frequent partiers. There were already enough rumors about Robert not being able to hold on to a woman, even with his enormous fortune and title. He didn't want the country to think he was threatened in any way, not especially by a man on his staff. Even a Greek god-looking man like Simon.

How's that working out for you so far? Robert chastised his overactive subconscious but silently admitted that maybe he was just a bit threatened. A bit.

When Simon's sportscar roared to life and sped off in the direction of the staff housing, raining dust and pebbles over Robert, he brushed them off and turned to Lorelai, a smile on his face.

"What the hell was that?" she demanded.

"I'm just checking to make sure you're okay. You looked like you could use a hand getting out of a sticky situation."

Okay, maybe that wasn't entirely true, but Robert didn't care. He'd gotten what he wanted. Lorelai alone, her "date" but a memory.

No longer concerned with her dress or how it hung on her perfect frame, Lorelai's hands set firmly on her hips. Robert knew she was aiming for defiant, but damn if the gesture didn't draw his gaze to her fleshy hips, make him desperate to run his hands over hers.

"Bullshit. How many times do I need to tell you off for you to understand that I don't want you?"

The blow to his gut like he'd been pounded by a heavyweight reverberated in Robert's chest. He'd been unclear himself about his interest in Lorelai—was it a simple attraction, or did he want more from her? But having her shut down any permutation that allowed him access to her stung.

Robert stood, feet planted, jaw set, knowing he was beat. She'd said it herself, she didn't want anything to do with him, and all the times he kept inserting himself into her life were just making him look like a fool. Under no circumstances would he give a woman—especially a woman like Lorelai—reason to think he was using his crown to force himself upon her.

He would not be the man who stole his brother's fiancé.

He'd back down—for now, until she had a chance to settle into her new position as not only the manager of the stables, but the owner/operator. Then he'd be her friend. Be there for her as a boss should be, not preying on her like a chump.

He shook his head, forced a smile. "How was your date?" he asked.

She threw him a glance that seared his heart, threatened daggers if he pursued that line of questioning. He tossed up his hands in an attempt to offer a peace treaty. Okay, so maybe the cooling-off period would be longer than he thought.

"I only hope you had a good time. I'm sorry if I ruined it."

When her gaze softened, almost imperceptibly, he let out a breath he hadn't realized he'd been holding in.

"It was fine. Simon's nice."

Robert nodded, all he could do while his teeth were clamped down on his tongue to prevent him from sharing what he really thought of the huntsman. His gaze was now pinned to the ground, nervous about keeping it on her ample hips and delectable chest and what that might do to his libido.

"And a braggart. And a little handsy, if I'm being honest," she added.

He looked back up at her, meeting her eyes, which were a soft green, not unlike the jade he'd collected for Marjorie early in their marriage on a diplomatic trip to China. She'd given it back to him when she'd left the castle, left it among other tokens of his love, including their daughter. What hurt him the most and tore him to pieces was that a year ago Ginny had stopped asking about her mother altogether and started in on Robert for just any mother. Someone to read her stories at night because Robert was getting the princesses' voices all wrong. He knew that was just the beginning, that there was so much more he was destined to get wrong if he didn't have help, a woman's gentle touch.

The problem was that in procuring a mother figure for his daughter, it would mean opening up his heart again, and he just wasn't sure he was ready for that.

Though as the emerald orbs looked into his soul, he found that statement not entirely truthful. Maybe he could be, if he found the right woman. One who could challenge him, ignite his passion. *One who actually wants to be around me.* It was more than a little unfortunate that the woman standing in front of him met the first two qualities and didn't fulfill the last.

"Well, you give the word and I'll have him fired. Better yet, hung from the rafters."

His resolve to leave her alone almost cracked when she smiled up at him.

"He's not that bad. He's not the guy for me, but he's a heckuva hunter, an even better rider."

"Yes, that's true. It's why we took him on. Will you be going out with him again?"

"No. Once was enough. He's too pretty for me, anyway."

Robert let loose a chuckle. "You like them rougher around the edges?" he teased.

"I like a man who doesn't use more hair product than I do, at least."

"Good point. Did you at least make him pay?"

"I'm not that out of practice. Besides, I've got to save for a property I just purchased. And I couldn't say no to creme brulee."

They both laughed, and Robert decided then and there that was enough for him. Just to see her happy, smiling.

He'd done too much damage to the girl to expect more from the woman who'd shown back up in her place.

"All right, well, you have a good night. I'll see you this week with the contract."

She nodded and turned back toward the set of stairs that led up to her apartment above the stables. As Robert followed suit on the path up to the castle, his heart pulled, wishing he could go back in time and shake some sense into his younger self, get him to not be such a prick to the younger Lorelai.

"Hey," she called. In a flash, he was back at her side.

"Yes?" He heard the desperation, the hope in his voice, and mentally flagellated himself for having such a hard time letting her go when she clearly didn't want him, and when he didn't even know what the pull to her stemmed from. Physical attraction? Yes, clearly. But was there something more, something deeper? Until he figured it out, he needed to keep his distance.

"Thanks for checking up on me. I haven't, um, dated much, and I have a feeling had you not come around, Simon might have had expectations I wasn't comfortable with."

"You're welcome," Robert replied, the huskiness in his tone a result of the fact that her scent—lilacs and vanilla—was close enough to put him in a lust-filled coma. *Christ.*

"Just don't think that gives you carte blanche to spy on me every time I go out." She poked him in the chest, but it was a playful gesture, met with twinkling eyes, and he resisted the urge to clasp her hand in his and pull her near, let her scent and mouth, envelop him.

"I wasn't—" he started, but when her eyebrows raised, he knew he'd never lie to her, not even to cover his own backside. "Okay. I promise. But do me a favor. Keep my private cell number in your phone in case you need it."

She nodded, her eyebrows still raised, but the smile wiped clean from her face. She pulled her phone from a small black clutch he hadn't noticed and handed it over to him. When he took it from her, his fingers brushed hers, and an electric charge sent shivers down his arm and to his core. An almost inaudible gasp from her said she felt it, too. *Interesting*.

With his number safe in her phone, Robert knew he had to walk away if he had any hope of saving face and working alongside this intoxicating woman.

"Have a good night, Lorelai," he whispered, pulling her hand to his lips for what he meant as a chivalrous, benign gesture. Instead, she trembled in his grasp and he felt shaken to his core.

He dropped her hand reluctantly and turned back for home. *Home*. He'd meant the castle, but for some reason when he thought of the word, an image of walking up the stairs with Lorelai flashed before him.

Each step toward the palace, his suite large enough to house most of the stables within its walls, his bed that he could roll over ten times in and still not reach the edge, had him wishing for a simpler life, one without the crown to encumber his every movement. For an instant that lingered in the air like lilac and vanilla, Robert considered giving it all up and running back to the stables, to his childhood friend, and showing her none of it mattered but her.

As he closed the castle door, though, Ginny ran up to him, her hair a fright, her face white as alabaster.

"Baby girl, what is it? You shouldn't be up this late."

"I had a nightmare. You were gone and I didn't know what to do."

Robert tucked his baby girl in his arms, sighing deep into the curls that reminded him of his mother.

"I'm here, now. And I'm not going anywhere again." As he uttered the words and felt them in his chest, he knew them to be true. His place was here, with his family, his country. It would do him a world of good not to forget that, but instead push the siren at the bottom of the path to the recesses of his mind and heart. She had no place up here, and as he'd promised his daughter, he wasn't going anywhere.

CHAPTER FIVE: THE PAST

Lorelai brushed down the gelding's hide, the dust wafting off him traveling up her nostrils and tickling them. She bit the end of her tongue to keep the sneeze at bay, then continued purring to the horse.

"You're so strong," she told Hercules, her father's last purchase before falling ill. She loved this horse for the memories he gave her, a gift she received each time she took him out for a ride, mucked his stall, cleaned his tack. He was old, wise, and seemed to understand that when she chose him for her afternoon jaunt, she needed a listening ear as well as a riding companion. He would often grumble back to her, giving her the distinct impression that he not only understood her, but had his own opinions on her out-loud musings.

"God, how I wish you were human. I could use your advice, Herc."

He blew her a raspberry, spraying her with saliva.

She laughed, thwacking him on the hide gently with the brush. "That's not nice. I need you to tell me what to do about a certain member of the royal staff."

Herc whinnied, eliciting another giggle from Lorelai.

"Yeah, him. He's frustrating, arrogant, and too darn

controlling. But he can be kind, understanding, and I don't know if you've noticed, but he's pretty handsome, too."

The horse grumbled, shaking his head.

"Fine." She chuckled, moving to his mane. "Maybe not to you. But if I told you the dreams I've been having about him, you'd blush."

"Who are you dreaming 'bout? And why are you talking to a horse?"

Lorelai screamed, never more thankful she was in a stall with Herc, who just moved to the corner of the pen instead of kicking or bucking. She knew better than to startle a horse, but the small voice from an invisible body had shocked her senseless.

For a split second, she imagined that she'd willed Herc into responding, then as her shock subsided, she called out, "Who's here?" Lord, she was going crazy if she thought a horse was talking to her. Probably a result of overworking herself to compensate for the time she'd been away. She tried to recall her last day off and couldn't pin down when she'd taken one. As soon as she was done for the day, she'd schedule one.

"Me. I wanna see BillieJean. I missed her."

Now that she had her bearings, Lorelai recognized the soft but commanding voice. It belonged to Ginny, Robert's daughter.

"Hey there, Ginny. You here alone?" She was no stranger to the little girl wandering her way, as she'd somehow escaped the palace twice a week and made her way to the stables, only to be picked up by a frazzled and apologetic member of the staff. Robert hadn't returned since the night she'd gone on the date with Simon. Lorelai wasn't sure that was the good thing she'd once imagined it was.

Every time she'd found Ginny in the stables, she'd hoped he'd be the one to come retrieve his daughter, but he seemed to have gotten the message that she didn't want him. Of course, that couldn't be further from the truth.

She wanted him desperately, her body calling out for him to follow through on the kiss they'd shared all those weeks ago. She just knew she couldn't have him the way she wanted—fully, completely—and wondered why she bothered with the wanting at all when she was well aware of his weaknesses.

One, he was a playboy—or at least he had been. The fact that his ex-wife was once engaged to the younger prince, then had left Robert after only two years of marriage didn't bode well for thinking Robert had grown in that department.

Two, and more importantly, he was a father—a single father with sole responsibility for the little girl who was wandering around looking for Billie Jean. Lorelai wasn't sure where she stood on kids, only that she wasn't over the loss of her parents, her father especially, and didn't want to think about adding a convoluted layer to her ability to process that with a child of her own. Or one she was responsible for.

Which led to the third and final issue—she had no idea if Robert's interests in her went beyond the physical attraction neither of them could deny pulsed through them when they were near each other. Loving him as long as she had would be a loss she would never recover from if she were to lose him again.

"Yes. 'Tricia didn't want to come and see the horses. I dunno why. They are the best!" Ginny squealed. Hercules grumbled as Lorelai left the stall and made her way to Ginny, who'd managed to corral one of the nameless barn cats, a black feral thing that was good at keeping mice at bay but not much in the way of cuddling. Ginny didn't seem to get the message, though, squeezing the poor thing within an inch of its life. Lorelai bet that cat wouldn't make the same mistake twice.

"They are the best, I agree. Now, we should talk about having a time each week that you come see me, and maybe I can talk your dad into letting you ride Billie Jean, but you have to promise me if I do that, you won't sneak down here anymore."

"Ooooh! I won't, I won't. I would love to ride BillieJean. But why were you talking to that other horse? Does he talk back to you?"

Lorelai had forgotten in her surprise to see the girl in her barn again that she'd been mumbling about Ginny's father. Lord, please let Ginny be too distracted to pay attention to that small detail.

"Um, no. He doesn't. But sometimes I need to talk to someone about something I'm feeling and I don't have a person with me. Hercules is a great listener, so I tell him instead. Do you ever do that?" Lorelai crossed her fingers behind her back in hopes that Ginny didn't hear *what* she was talking about.

"I talk to my doll, Judy like that. I tell her how I want a mommy. Kinda like how you want a husband."

Lorelai almost fell off the stool she was on. She knew her cheeks were a cherry red by the heat they emanated.

"What do you mean?" she asked, her face turned from Ginny in the hopes of hiding her mortification of being so aptly seen by an almost-four-year-old.

"You were talking to your horse about a boy. I think you like him, even though you said not nice things about him. 'Tricia said if you don't have anything nice to say, you should keep your mouth shut, but you said nice things, too, so I won't tell her."

Lorelai had met Patricia, the head of house up at the palace, and was glad Ginny wouldn't share her thought with the woman as comfortable with gossip as a talk show host.

"Thanks, Ginny," Lorelai said. She stepped off the small stool, her knees wobbling. She'd shucked hay a thousand times in her life, maybe more, but today she felt like an amateur in more ways than one. "I appreciate you not saying anything about the mean things I said about the boy I like, but you should know I'll never ask you to keep secrets for me, okay? I'd like you to know we can talk about anything that's bothering you, though. That's part of why I love horses and riding so much. Because I can think about life and how to solve my problems while I'm here, or in the fields with Billie Jean."

She'd never done the "kid" thing, wasn't sure she'd ever wanted to after losing her mom so early, but this little girl made it easy. Ginny was so sweet, so damn honest, Lorelai had the feeling she was talking to one of her friends, not a preschooler.

"Thanks. That's what 'Tricia says, too. You're real nice, Lor-y-lai. I wish you were my mom."

A smile cracked Lorelai's cheeks, splitting her heart in two. She knew it was just the fact that Lorelai was Ginny's connection to Billie Jean, but the sentiment was so simply stated, it shot straight through Lorelai's chest.

"You're pretty great, too, Ginny. So, why don't we head up the hill and see if we can talk to Patricia about having you down here to ride every so often." A jolt of excitement rose in her chest at the thought of sharing her love of horses with a girl young enough to learn, yet old enough to "get it," and with the financial means to keep up the practice as long as she desired. If her father hadn't worked the private stables for the royal family, she never would have had the opportunity to pursue the types of riding she had. Teaching Ginny would be an incredible experience for them both.

"Patricia is gone. But we can ask my aunt Aury. She's 'sposed to be watching me at lunch."

"Perfect. Say bye to Billie Jean and we'll walk up."

While Ginny thought she was sneaking sugar cubes to Billie Jean—using a sleight of hand trick Lorelai herself had thought she'd invented when she was Ginny's age—Lorelai thought about what it would mean to be a mother, more specifically a stepmother. Her own mother had only been able to give three years of her love and knowledge to Gregory, only minutes to Lorelai, before she passed away, leaving Gregory and her to be raised by a single father—not unlike Robert having to raise Ginny on his own. Her father had never remarried, nor expressed an interest in the idea.

It wasn't an ideal situation for any of them, nor had her childhood been perfect, but she'd loved how close she and her father had grown before he sent her to America to study. God, how she missed him. Would Ginny miss the time alone with her father if he ever remarried? Would she resent him for bringing another woman into her life when they'd been getting along fine? When Ginny was a teenager, would she rebel against a mother-figure who wasn't hers by birth?

There were so many questions tumbling around in her head, but none of the answers surfaced. They were contingent on time and circumstances that weren't even present. Lorelai was so lost in the unsettling thoughts that when someone tapped her on the shoulder, she almost screamed again.

Whipping around, she found herself face to face with the most stunning woman she'd ever seen. She was shorter than Lorelai, but curvy in all the ways that mattered to most men. Despite only coming up to Lorelai's shoulder, her legs were long, tanned like she spent her time in the sun. Her hair was the same chestnut color as Lorelai's, but instead of being long and unruly like Lorelai's was, it was cut in a long bob. Suddenly, Lorelai was ten years old again, jealousy creeping up her spine at the way the cut effortlessly and stylishly framed the woman's exotic features. It was as discomforting as it was when she was younger.

"Um, hi. Can I help you?" Lorelai was usually confident, found other women inspiring rather than intimidating, but for some reason, this petite pixie made her feel like she was a loafing giant, unfamiliar with her own body and the clunky way it moved.

"You must be the new stable manager. I'm Aurelia,

Philip's wife. I've been excited to meet you, see if maybe I can talk you into a ride sometime. Not until this little guy joins us, of course, but when he does and I have my body back, I'd love to hit the trails with you."

In a matter of four sentences, Lorelai dropped all of her preconceptions of the woman and felt instantly at ease with her. Her accent was as much home to Lorelai as the longer vowels of Aldonian. *New York.* Hers would always be a complicated relationship with the city, as it had given her the knowledge that made her an expert in her field, a field she adored, but it had also stolen away precious time she could have spent with her father. It would be nice to hear that accent, though, from time to time.

Not to mention that in her initial once-over of Aurelia, Lorelai had completely missed the now-impossibly obvious swell of Aurelia's stomach. It was the only indication that the woman was pregnant, though, the rest of her as compact as her stature. Some women had all the luck…

"Hi, I'm Lorelai. Nice to meet you. This little one and I were actually just about to come find you." Lorelai gestured to the tuft of hair that gave away Ginny's hiding spot by Billie Jean's stall. Aurelia laughed, a light sound that perfectly suited her.

"That little escape artist. She's a pro."

"That she is. I actually wanted to talk to you all about having her down here once or twice a week to play with Billie Jean, maybe even ride with me. Do you think that could work?"

"Wow. She'd love that. Can you spare the time?"

"For that girl, I can. Seems we're going to be hanging out down here together either way, so I figured why not make it happen above board."

Both women seemed to notice the way Ginny inched toward them at the talk of her having regular visits with the horses. Lorelai didn't miss the excitement, the nerves on the young girl's face. It was the same with her as a child. Riding was as essential to her as breathing.

"I like your thinking. I'll talk to Robert, but it should be fine. He's traveling a lot this week, anyway, so I'll just make sure Patricia gives the okay. Would you mind if we brought my daughter, Noelle?"

"Noelle, like the former queen?"

"Yes, Philip adored her, so there wasn't a more fitting name for the gift that brought he and I together."

"I agree, and I'd love to have her, too. So, um, where is the King traveling to this week?" She'd tried for cool, collected, mildly curious, but what she gave off was shrill obsession, her voice an octave higher than it should be.

Lorelai caught the knowing grin that stretched across Aurelia's alabaster skin.

"Robert's in the Republic of Georgia, the lucky devil. Their wine makes me wish I could go with them and that it was a month from now so I could drink my weight."

"Them?" Lorelai asked, busying her hands with flaking off more hay for the new gelding in the far stall. She'd keep her words to a minimum until she could calm her body's reaction at the mention of the King.

"He and Philip. Some amnesty project. He's glad you're home by the way." There was definitely no mistaking the meaning behind the wink Aurelia threw her way.

"Philip? He and I were good friends, but he was always closer to Gregory. Those two and their shenanigans..." She trailed off, thinking about the three young men in her life—her brother. Philip. *Robert*. When they were younger, there was no denying they would be a force to be reckoned with. Now, that was clearly the case, as they each seemed to have found their niche in doing their part for their country. It wouldn't be long until Lorelai carved hers out for herself as well.

"Not Philip. Robert. He gets these little cherry-red circles on his cheeks when he talks about you. He tries to play it cool, kinda like you just did, but he's all nerves when it comes to you."

Lorelai didn't know what to do, what to say about that

new information. He'd been keeping his distance—like she'd demanded—and hadn't so much as come to retrieve his daughter when she made one of her runs for the stables.

Lorelai had been happy about that at first, but there was no denying the distraction that he caused with his absence. Now that he'd taken her less-than-subtle clues to leave her alone, she couldn't shake him from her thoughts. Damned if she did, or if she didn't. Great.

Her heart sped up and moisture dampened the space between her thighs as she let her thoughts wander to the red cheeks Aurelia had described. She knew them well. Robert, brilliant businessman as he was, hid his emotions about as well as an elephant stalking a mouse.

"Um, well, I'm sure he's just glad I'm taking over for my dad. He's a tough act to follow."

Aurelia giggled. "Yeah, I'm sure that's it. You know, if you two got out of your own way, you'd actually be kinda great together."

Again, Lorelai was at a loss for words. It was all she'd wanted as a young woman. Even as an adult in New York she'd dreamt about the man coming to claim her from the city. But the truth was more complicated than that. It had always been a one-sided love, and she was better off with her new business, training to take over the hunt, putting her energy where it might reap rewards.

"That ship sailed a long time ago," Lorelai said, a weak smile turning the corners of her lips.

"Ships come back to port eventually. They're always in need of a safe harbor."

Aurelia grabbed Lorelai in an embrace that felt at once awkward and comfortable, like she'd known the woman five years, not just five minutes. She settled into it, realizing how starved she was for human contact in general.

"Thank you," Lorelai said. "For letting Ginny come down and, you know, the rest."

Aurelia winked and turned back to find her charge, who was back at it with the barn cat. Apparently, the cat wasn't as interested in her own survival as Lorelai thought.

"See you this week. Does Friday work for the girls to come down?"

"Friday is lovely. Would you like to grab lunch afterward?"

"I'll check my schedule, but a girls' date is in order soon either way." With that, the woman turned on her heels and, with Ginny's hand wrapped lovingly in hers, walked out as quietly as she'd come in.

The rest of the week passed quickly, with a new pair of geldings added to the team, as well as the final training of her barn staff. Lorelai lost herself in the work from just before sunrise until long after sunset, when she'd close out her day with an American beer. On Thursday night, she barely made it up the stairs to her apartment without using the handrails her father had attached when he got sick. Her knees wobbled under the stress of four of the longest, most arduous workdays she'd ever had, her thighs burning with exertion. What she wouldn't give for a pair of strong, knowing hands to rub each of her muscles that screamed.

She settled instead for a hot shower, letting the near-scalding water pulse over her shoulders, relieving some of the tension. Afterward, she shimmied into her robe, added thick wool socks, and went straight to bed, the bottle of wine she'd planned for herself forgotten on the counter.

As she fell off into sleep, her last conscious thoughts were of the barn she was slowly—and not without great effort—making her own. A thin smile was pressed to her lips as she let herself succumb to slumber, knowing how proud her father would be if he was there to see what she'd done. New fencing along the southern border of the corral, the outdoor arena was almost complete, dressage-ready. Not to mention the gelding brothers she'd broken in enough to take for a trail ride that afternoon. It wasn't easy riding, but she'd enjoyed the time from the barn, the escape into the beautiful fall countryside. Aldonia did some things well; she gave her home country credit there.

With that, she was asleep and didn't rouse the next morning until she heard a sharp rapping on the door. In her half-dreaming state, she imagined it was her cranky landlord in New York, always on her about the odd hours she kept. He'd assumed she was an escort—or worse— and was confused why she never brought any men home. She'd never corrected him, not until the last week she was there and she invited him to the country ranch she'd been working on for the four years of her doctorate. His surprise had shown in his eyes, his loose jaw, and she'd relished that moment of righteousness more than was kind or necessary.

When the rapping came again, louder this time, she awoke more fully, taking in the very not-New York scenery.

"I'm coming," she yelled. Her voice was scratchy, and as she swung her heavy legs over the side of the bed, her body wasn't faring much better.

Ooooh. That hurt. Lorelai twisted, her back cracking three times before her feet planted, and she slowly made her way to the door. She must look like she'd spent her night tackling raccoons, but oh well. Most of the staff had seen her worse off at the end of each long day. She didn't care what she looked like as long as whoever was at the door was brandishing a coffee.

She cursed under her breath and took back that promise the moment she swung the door open, rougher than was called for. There, two cups of coffee in his hands—something that should have had Lorelai ushering him in with enthusiasm—was Robert, in jeans, riding boots, and a loose-fitting chambray unbuttoned halfway down his broad chest.

Lorelai screamed and ran for the bathroom, hoping the noise she heard come from him wasn't laughter. What the Sam Hell was he doing there, in her minuscule apartment?

She could die of embarrassment if her stomach didn't clench at the aroma of coffee and a heady cologne that made her dizzy.

"Aren't you going to invite me in?" he called. Though, she could hear from the heavy steps echoing on her wood floor he'd taken that liberty without any invitation from her. It figured.

"What are you doing here?" She turned the water to the shower on as hot as she could take it while she raked a toothbrush over her mouth. She jumped in the shower and bit her tongue as the water scalded her. Well, she was awake now.

"You're taking the girls riding, right? Or do you want me to bring them back later?"

"No, no, that's the plan, but they weren't coming until ten."

"It's ten-fifteen."

Lorelai froze, her hands lathered with shampoo, tangled in her hair.

"No. It can't be. I never sleep that long."

Now she was sure it was laughter she heard from the other side of the door. *Damn him. If he knew what I've been doing this week, he wouldn't dare scoff at me.* Besides, what did he know about hard, physical labor? She wondered when her body would have allowed her to wake up if left to its own devices. She almost thanked him until she heard the amusement from the other side of the bathroom door.

"I can bring them back if you need time to get ready."

Ha. She wouldn't give him the satisfaction at having caught her unprepared.

"No, I'll be out in a minute." She didn't mean to sound as clipped as she did, but with the way she was roused, and the lack of coffee in her system, nice was a long way off. "So, where is Aurelia? I thought she was bringing them?"

"I sent her and Philip away for the weekend. A baby-moon I think they call it. He's been working hard, and she's been doing far more than she should. So, Patricia and

I have the girls until Monday."

The frustration that had been bubbling at the back of Lorelai's throat, threatening to spill over in some even less-kind words, abated. That was a sweet gesture, one she was sure the couple appreciated. After all, in less than a month, it wouldn't be just the three of them anymore. Something inside her uncoiled at the thought of the family being built, the idea of an infant swaddled and embraced by Philip and his wife. It was an unfamiliar emotion that surfaced, akin to jealousy, but different. More powerful. It was almost an ache.

She'd address that later. Right now, she had a bigger problem, and he was holding a coffee for her on the other side of the wall.

"That's nice. So, um, where are the girls? You can just leave them with me. I'm sure you've got plenty on your plate, especially with Philip away." She was suddenly hyperaware of the thin slab of wood that separated her naked, water-dappled body from the man who'd occupied her heart and thoughts for as long as she could remember.

"Patricia's on her way down with them. I thought I'd precede them with coffee."

Oh, God. His voice was against the door. She wanted to tell him he could wait downstairs for her, but her voice lodged in her throat. "Besides, I think a ride in the countryside would do me well. You don't mind if I join, do you?"

If only she could unstick her voice, explain all the reasons that was a very bad idea. As she thought about how she might be able to come up with an excuse to duck him, she knew that even if she could turn away the king, she'd find it impossible to turn down the man.

"No, sure. Fine. That's fine." Oh, good. Her words became unstuck and vomited themselves all over him. Tossing on a thin flannel and some of her more comfortable riding jeans, she looked in the mirror. Something was missing. Though she'd never normally doll up for a ride, or anything other than a date, she carefully opened her drawer, hoping to be as quiet and as quick as she could. She added a thin layer of lip gloss and mascara, and finally satisfied that she at least wasn't the troll who'd all but slammed the door in the King's face, opened the bathroom door.

He'd made his way to the middle of the room, to her bedside, a visual that threw her heart into tumult. His knee rested atop her unmade mattress, while his strong hands grasped the one and only photo she kept in her apartment. It had captured her father and mother swinging Gregory, her mother late in her pregnancy with Lorelai, the look of joy captured on each of their faces. Though the photo faced Robert, she could have recreated it just from memory. Her mother hadn't known it then, but she'd only survived another month. Lorelai kept that photo out to remind herself what she'd cost her father, her brother, how much she owed them both for taking their favorite person from the Earth.

"I miss him," he admitted. "I never had a chance to get to know her, but he was like a father to Philip and me when we needed it most."

Lorelai's eyes welled up at the admission. Her ability to find fault in the man was wavering with each passing second.

"I ache every day for him. Her, too, but it's different. I was a newborn."

He took a step toward her, the photo still in his hands. His gaze cut through her, unraveled the coil further, amplifying the ache from earlier. Were they connected, her ache at the mention of family, and her every reaction to Robert's gaze?

"Yes, but a daughter needs her mother, no matter how old she gets. There's only so much a dad can understand." A wry smile touched the corners of Robert's lips.

She agreed with him on principle, recalling having to go to her dad when she'd woken up one morning to discover small breasts had sprouted seemingly overnight. He'd flushed and called Patricia, who'd taken her shopping for her first set of bras, admonishing him for being a prude in the process. There were more of those memories than she'd thought, and all of them came crashing against her at once.

Starting her period, going on her first date.

Needing to talk about her growing love for a man who didn't know she existed.

"Hmm. You're right there. You're doing a fine job with Ginny, though."

He chuckled, a humorless sound that echoed off her narrow walls.

"Sure. But she needs more. It'd be easier if she didn't ask for a mother every day. I'm not sure what to tell her anymore, honestly." He coughed, cleared his throat, and if Lorelai didn't know better, she'd say he was embarrassed at having shared so much about himself. "Today's the first day she hasn't said a word about it. I think you may have excited it right out of her."

"It's the horses. I was just as infatuated when I was her age."

Robert had somehow closed the distance between them, his chest only inches from hers. She struggled to breathe, afraid the scent that had stayed branded in her memory since their first kiss would infiltrate her senses and send her thoughts—and God-forbid her actions—to the gutter.

"No, it's you. She's taken with you. Not that I blame her." His breath was laced with mint. Combined with the heady musk—regal and all male—wafting off him, Lorelai was light-headed.

"Um, coffee? You said you have coffee?"

Her words had the desired effect. He stepped back and laughed. He put the picture back on her bed stand and retrieved the two paper cups he'd left by the entrance. With the small distance between them, Lorelai could feel her thoughts unfreezing, her breath regulate. Her limbs followed, accepting the cup of coffee he held out for her.

"Let's head on down. I wouldn't want the girls to think we're not going."

"Well, hey," he said, grabbing her wrist with his free hand, "I've got the papers here for you to sign if you're interested."

Shockwaves of heat traveled up her arm from where his hand held hers, firm but gentle. They raged in her chest, hot and powerful reminders of the intimate kiss they'd shared, a kiss she'd replayed in her head a thousand times since, wishing it had gone on for days.

The only thing that stopped Lorelai in her tracks, abated the heat that roiled like an inferno in her chest, were the papers he pulled folded from his back pocket. If she signed them, she'd be the owner of the barn, the apartment, the piece of land she rode each day. It was almost too much. Too good.

"Should I have my lawyer look over them?"

"You may, of course, but there is a clause at the top of page one that lets you break the contract within the first month if both parties aren't happy with the arrangement. Including the payment schedule. Lorelai," he started, his hand dropping to hers and grasping it. "I'd really like to forgive the loan. Please just let this be a gift. It's far overdue."

"That's more than fair, Robert, thank you." It was, too. She'd never get a better offer, of that she was certain. It was the way her body reacted to him that gave her pause. If she accepted his offer, she'd never be free of him. "But I need to do this on my own. I'll write you the first check now in exchange for the deed to the property, with a lien, of course."

He sighed, and she caught a hint of regret in his exhale, his breath warm on her chest. Why couldn't he see that she was doing this to protect herself, her brother? If she earned this, she'd put more of herself into it than if it was just handed to her. That was what life had taught her so far, albeit the hard way.

"Here's a pen. If you change your mind, Lorelai, please tell me. I've done enough damage to you for one lifetime. Let me start to make up for it."

She took the pen he offered, and this time, when her skin grazed his, she didn't feel heat, but calm take her over and settle in her stomach. She nodded, and without giving it the thought it required, she signed each of the ten pages, initialed half a dozen lines. Her father would take her to task for signing such an important, life-altering contract without at least giving it her undivided attention. He'd have demanded a lawyer as well, but there was nothing in her over-sensitive gut that warned her off the deal, off Robert.

She went to her desk drawer, once her mother's, and scribbled out a check for the first mortgage payment. A flutter of excitement coursed through her. She was finally doing it. Everything she'd sacrificed would be worth it now that her dreams were coming to fruition. Well, almost everything. Only the absence of her father made the air around her heavy, somber.

"Okay, Lorelai, you're now the proud owner of the stables, including twenty geldings, three mates, and one soon-to-be foal. I'll have this processed with my office this afternoon and a copy sent your way when it's complete." He shook her hand, and the weight of the deal settled in the palm of her hand.

"Thank you," she said, heat building behind her eyes. "Um, let's go meet the girls." She added the last part in a desperate attempt to keep her composure. Tonight, in the privacy of her apartment, she could pore over the contract with a bottle of wine and cry to her heart's content if she wanted.

But not now. Not here.

He nodded and took her hand as they descended the steps. Outside, the bright near-afternoon light assaulted

Lorelei's vision. She focused her blurry gaze on a lightning-quick ball of kinetic energy barreled toward her, realizing it was Ginny as the girl threw herself into Lorelei's arms. Lorelai squeezed her tightly, the events from moments ago washing off her, replaced by a growing affection for the child.

"Oooh," Ginny squealed in Lorelai's left ear, "I can't believe I get to ride BillieJean! This is the best day of my liiiiife!" Her pitch was operatic, and Lorelai couldn't help but laugh at the child's enthusiasm. It was all she needed to wake up properly. Well, that and the coffee from Robert she still held.

As Lorelai put Ginny down so she could chase the poor barn kitten who by now had resigned herself to the fate of being loved to death, Lorelai noticed a more reticent little girl in the back of the barn. She walked over to her as Patricia and Robert talked about the girls' afternoon nap schedules. Their voices dropped to almost a whisper when Lorelai walked by. What were they up to?

She shifted her focus to the girl before her, an almost-clone of the young woman Lorelai had met earlier in the week. Both children, though stunning in the way of child models, with porcelain skin, heart-shaped lips, and globe-like orbs for eyes, looked nothing like their equally-handsome fathers, save the soft blue of Ginny's eyes and the Caribbean-blue-green of the other little girl's. Lorelai's imagination drifted to a third little girl with her chocolate-brown cascade of curls and Robert's eyes.

Where had that image come from? Either way, it shook her to her core, bringing back the now-familiar ache in her abdomen.

"Hi, there. I'm Lorelai. You must be Noelle."

The child pinned her gaze to the ground but let loose a small nod. The hilarity of the disparity between the two cousins didn't escape Lorelai. For every bit Ginny was outgoing, talkative, one might even say adorably invasive, her cousin was shy, quiet, and reticent.

"Well, I'm excited you were able to come along on a ride with us this morning. Do you like horses?"

At this question, Noelle's head popped up, her eyes wide but no longer filled with fright. She nodded.

"Good." Lorelai laughed. There was at least one similarity between the girls. "Would you like to meet your horse?" Noelle nodded again, her small hand finding its way into Lorelai's. Lorelai couldn't suppress the grin that spread from her cheeks to her eyes as she walked Noelle down to Hercules. This was good. It was just what she needed.

Robert was there with Ginny, who held out a carrot for the greedy horse.

"Did Patricia leave?"

"She did. She sends you her best, and let me know there are cookies in Ginny's backpack for the trail."

Lorelai's mouth watered on instinct. She was hungry, having skipped breakfast in lieu of riding with the family, but even if she was stuffed to the brim, she would find room for Patricia's cookies. The soft-centered ginger molasses were her favorite as a child, and though she scoured the city, she'd never found their equal in New York, nor anywhere else she traveled.

"Ginger molasses?"

"And peanut butter."

"Dang. Okay, well, let's get this show on the road. You've got Dexter, who you should know has healed nicely since you last met. He had a nice little abscess that needed attending to after you stole him from the barn." Though she teased him, no mirth crept into her voice. Somewhere along the way, she'd forgiven Robert for the injury to her horse, amongst other sins. "I think it would be best if you took Noelle with you." She glanced down at the girl who'd transferred her vise grip to Robert's hand.

"Yeah, I'm sorry about that. Glad Dexter's doing better. He's had a great doc." He winked, and as Lorelai's cheeks burned with the compliment, the crest between her thighs dampened. She coughed, cleared the air of the lust she felt lingering there. They were there for the kids, not romance. "Anyway, taking Noelle seems like the best option."

"Are you okay with me taking Ginny, then?"

"Of course. Lorelai, I trust you implicitly." His hand rested on her shoulder, and though the calm from earlier remained, the heat was back, igniting and setting her ablaze. Good Lord, would she ever be capable of a benign conversation with this man?

As Lorelai set about gathering the saddles and bridles for the two horses, she kept her gaze on Robert with the two girls, one propped up on each of his hips so they could pet Billie Jean. He laughed as they tried to stick carrot sticks up his nose, his voice echoing off the thick barn walls while he tickled his daughter and niece. They squealed with joy, a sound so authentic and genuine, it was hard to be around them and not be happy.

And she realized she was. Happy. For maybe the first time since her father had passed away.

Robert's striated shoulders, ripped with taut muscles that flexed under the weight of the preschoolers, pulled at his shirt, and the heat that still warmed Lorelai from the inside drifted south. Okay, so maybe she was more than a little happy.

How had she gone from not seeing the man in weeks, only to be there in her newly-owned barn, readying him and his family for a trail ride like it was the most natural thing in the world? Dueling emotions of lust and fear warred within her mind, but she pushed past both to see the day for what it was—a ride with her former boss and his kids.

It was that simple, wasn't it?

Mounting Billie Jean, circling her arms around Ginny, she caught Robert's gaze and saw confusion muddle his expression. She repeated the *it's a simple ride* mantra, though when his cheeks pinkened and his eyes filled with the lust she'd witnessed with their first kiss, she worried that maybe this time, the situation wasn't as black and white. It definitely wasn't as simple as she hoped.

What, then, was it?

She hoped she had the time and courage to figure things out this time around.

CHAPTER SIX: THE FIRST TIME

Robert tried to keep his gaze on the trail in front of him, but damn if Lorelai bouncing along beside him, her hips and breasts rising and falling with each trot of the horse wasn't driving him to distraction. He felt like a lecherous creep lusting that way about a woman who had his daughter on her lap, but that was part of it. When Lorelai would lean down, whisper in Ginny's ear, and his daughter would beam back up at her chaperone, Robert filled with more than just simple physical attraction for Lorelai.

God help him, but he found himself *wanting* for the first time since his daughter was born.

Something in his chest shook, broke free of the usual tightness constraining his every movement. When it settled again, he recognized it as admiration, something he hadn't felt with Marjorie. It was close to another feeling he dared not give a name to yet, and that surprised the hell out of him.

Sure, he'd wanted a mother figure for Ginny, someone the girl could look up to, learn to love, but he'd never expected his own reaction when that happened. Or how mesmerizing he would find the woman Ginny chose.

Wasn't it Ginny who'd led him back to Lorelai? His head-strong daughter couldn't be kept from the stables, which was more than a little responsible for carting him to the doorstep of a woman he both craved and repelled. Not a winning combination. But still, an alluring one.

"Daddy, look!" Ginny's failed attempt at a whisper shook him from his thoughts. He raised his head to see they'd ridden to the grove with the small creek he'd followed Lorelai to last time they'd ridden together. He smiled over at his daughter, but the simple gesture belied the roaring fire that spread from Robert's chest to his lips, that heated with the memory of the last time he and Lorelai were there.

The kiss.

Her hands fisted in his hair.

He'd been a goner then, just hadn't known it until now.

"It's beautiful, Ginny." His gaze trailed down the dips and valleys of the woman who reached up and carefully set his daughter safely on solid ground. He did the same with his niece, unable to pull his gaze from the curves and muscles that worked together in one stunning form to tie the horses up.

Beautiful didn't begin to cover it.

"Daaad-y, I mean look at BillieJean. She's eating! She likes grass. Gross."

Lorelai laughed, and Robert followed suit. God, he wanted to make it so Lorelai laughed all the time, if only so he could selfishly hear the way it met the breeze, added light to the waning fall sun.

"She likes grass like you and I like salad. It's good for her." Lorelai grabbed a handful of leafy greens and held out her hand, palm flat, so Billie Jean could feast.

Ginny copied her, reaching far above her shoulder so her arm could get close enough to the horse's mouth.

"I don't like salad. Yuck. But maybe it's like brock-leep. I like that when Patricia makes it."

Lorelai shot Robert a look that begged explanation. He

chuckled.

"She means Patricia's cheese and broccoli. There's nothing melted cheese doesn't make edible."

Lorelai laughed again, and Robert's heart swelled at his ability to put a smile on the woman's face, when for so long all he'd given her was a deeper scowl. Maybe that meant the growing seed of friendship had hope of turning into more. Patricia had long said he needed a woman in his life. He agreed, finally. But not just any woman. Only one would do.

"There's nothing Patricia doesn't make edible, you mean."

"Agreed. Anyway, speaking of the prodigal baker, this seems like a nice enough place to sit and enjoy the c-o-o-k-i-e-s she sent with us."

"Cookies!" Ginny squealed, Noelle joining in the high-pitched reverie when she caught on.

It was Robert's turn to laugh, a sound that came from his chest, further shaking loose the stones of regret that had held him down for so long. It felt good to be outside, to laugh, to watch a beautiful woman with his daughter. Simple pleasures he'd missed.

"I guess that's the end of s-p-e-l-l-i-n-g. And time to fire her tutor. I thought I had another two years of hiding treats and profanity from her."

The smile that took over Lorelai's face reached her eyes, brightening them even more if that was possible.

"She's incredibly intelligent. You can see it in the way she is with the horses. She's mature beyond her years."

"God help us. She must get it from her mother."

Lorelai shook her head. Robert watched as a tendril sprung loose from the front of her ponytail and fought the urge to tuck it behind her ear. Even a simple gesture like that he didn't trust himself with. She ignited him with the smallest brush of her skin against his; touching her face would set him ablaze in a way he didn't think he'd recover from.

"No, I'm pretty sure it's all from her father."

Robert's chest rumbled and shook with the compliment that bordered on flirting. More stones fell and didn't settle back this time. He felt loose, free.

"Thank you. Hey girls, first one to the beach at the creek gets an extra cookie," he called out, tossing Lorelai a wink. He didn't miss the crimson that crept across her chest and up her cheeks. Jesus, he wished he could touch the spot that he was responsible for heating up.

Instead, in desperate need of a distraction, he tore after the girls, whose laughter and screams turned feverish the closer he got to them. All three of them reached the water at the same time, breathless from the laughter they could barely contain more so than the exertion. When water splashed him square across the face, he looked up to see Lorelai across the creek from him, a look of mischief in her features, her hands glistening with moisture.

"How—" he started.

"A small footbridge just over there. My dad built it for me when I was a kid. It's a shortcut to town. And to the beach, which means I get the extra cookie." She held out her hand, a smile that spoke of mischief. Eyes that glittered with more of the same.

Ginny and Noelle voiced their protestations, claiming the cookie for their own. Lorelai took the bag with the treats from her back and made her way back across the bridge Robert had somehow missed. He was missing so much. It was time to slow down, appreciate the small things.

"Okay, I'll split my winnings with you girls, but you have to do me a favor." Their wide stares stuck on the cookie Lorelai procured, combined with their eager nods, told Robert they'd do just about anything for Lorelai at that moment. Horses and cookies had gained her two friends for life.

He sat back with a cookie of his own, his forearms propping him up on the dew-laden grass. It was cool and contrasting with the heat of the fall sun beating down on him. Robert was completely at peace watching the three ladies whisper and giggle and enjoy their cookies. He shut his eyes and turned his face to the sun, letting the moment wash over him, strip him of the stress of the unanswered questions that rolled in the back of his mind.

When the first drop of water splashed his cheek, he looked up again, expecting storm clouds building above them. When nothing but the blue of the day stared back, he wheeled around, and there, with drinking cups from the backpack filled to the brim with creek water, were the three ladies, matching fire in each of their eyes.

"No, no, no." He shook his head as he stood, and despite the inevitability of the oncoming attack, could even see a couple of defensive maneuvers he could work to avoid the onslaught. Still, the smile didn't leave his face.

"Yes, Daddy. Oooh, you're gonna get it!"

He laughed and scooped up his daughter, water tumbling over them both, his laughter blending with hers in a harmony he wasn't sure they'd ever shared. When was the last time he'd held his daughter like this? Played with her, not let her play around him? God, it felt good.

"Help!" she squealed between fits of laughter. Billie Jean grumbled behind him, and as he put Ginny back down and turned to check on the horse, he was met with a face full of water.

When his vision cleared, water cascading down his nose and chin, Lorelai was there, blocking the two girls, her cup empty. Her gaze danced, and her chest heaved with tampered laughter. If it was the last thing he did that day, he'd get it out of her.

"You… you," he said. But he couldn't finish that sentence with the gravity he wanted. Not even his eyes could hide the liquid heat he felt for the woman in front of him.

"What about me?" she challenged.

He'd have bet his limitless fortune that the look she

sent him, the one that pierced his heart and caused a swelling in his groin at the same time, burned with the same fire. He took a step toward her, the girls skipping back to the horses by then. Lorelai's eyes widened, and she stumbled backward.

Suddenly, he caught a glimpse of the girl she'd been before he'd gotten a hold of her, destroying her confidence. He'd been selfish back then, but not anymore. He'd never let her feel anything less than the wonder she was.

He reached out, caught her with his arm, but the wet grass beneath them won the battle, and he and Lorelai tumbled to the ground. At least the soft earth that caught them was forgiving, especially because he landed on top of her with the full brunt of his weight.

"Crap," he mumbled, patting her hips, her legs. "Are you okay?"

She didn't answer right away, and the breath he'd been holding in caught in his chest. He'd hurt her. If he did, he'd never forgive himself. Cupping a hand beneath her neck, he started to roll off of her until her arm snagged him in place. He only had a moment for the confusion to register in his eyes before her arm simultaneously pulled him down to her, and her up to him.

Within a second, her lips were on his, hot and hungry. Muscle memory took over, and his body reacted to hers like they hadn't spent weeks apart. His mouth opened for her, his tongue meeting hers halfway. She tasted like chocolate and mint, and he made a mental note to thank Patricia for the gift of her cookies that somehow were made even more magical when combined with Lorelai's natural flavor.

He groaned against her as her hips rose to meet his, grinding against his now half-erect shaft. Jesus, this woman made him hard just imagining her. Now, her body laid out along his, he wasn't sure why he hadn't come at the first taste of her lips. He pulled her bottom lip into his mouth and nibbled on it.

"Ew, gross! They're *kissing*!" Ginny squealed.

Robert broke off from Lorelai, regret instantly settling in his chest as he put as much distance between them as possible.

"We, um, were, just, um—" he started, but Ginny and Noelle ran off, tittering about how "grown-ups are weird" before he could put words to what they'd seen. Sure, it was vanilla, nothing more than a passionate kiss between two consenting adults, but in another couple of seconds, he knew where he'd have liked it to go, and the worst thing was, he hadn't given a thought to his daughter and niece once his lips had sealed against Lorelai's. She was a shot of his father's moonshine come to life—mind-effing-altering with just a sip.

"Should we head back?" she asked. Her voice was thick with the same desire coursing through him. She was looking down at the ground, her cheeks now flushed with the heat they'd shared, and he was pretty sure the same mortification he felt at being caught by the girls.

"Hey," he said, tipping her cheek up to meet him. "There's nothing to be embarrassed about. I, um, I liked that. A lot."

That was the understatement of the century.

"Yeah, but Ginny—" she began.

"Will be fine," he finished. "Let's get them back, and then can I take you out to dinner? No, scratch that. I'm taking you out. No excuses."

The two seconds of silence before Lorelai answered him felt like an eternity. He liked this woman, was drawn to her in a way that didn't make any sense given his history with her and his position as King. But he understood her reticence spoken aloud in the pause. He was a single dad, the ruler of a kingdom. Not to mention the fact that he'd treated her like crap their entire young adulthood. The fact that she even gave him the time of day spoke volumes to her character.

"I'd like that," she said, so softly he wasn't sure he'd heard her correctly.

"Good. Good," he said, unable to make it past those two words. He hadn't figured on her saying yes; he'd prayed for it, yes, but never in a million years thought she'd consent. "Um, I'll gather the girls and call ahead to Patricia to come grab them."

"I'll ready the horses. They should be well-fed and watered by now," she replied.

He watched her walk away, the way her hips swayed, almost as if to music he couldn't hear. When she looked back over her shoulder at him, her eyes and smile luminescent, it was all he could do not to toss the girls over his shoulders and sprint back to the castle with or without the horses. He'd been a single father for over three years now, and though he had Patricia and a slew of helpful staff, it was to aid him in parenting so he could work. He couldn't recall the last time he'd shrugged his duties as a father or a king to simply be Robert.

Until that moment, he hadn't considered it possible.

The ride back to the castle was a quiet one, the girls both exhausted and ready for their afternoon naps. Robert made sure his horse, Dexter, sidled up next to Billie Jean and Lorelai each time the trail widened. At one such place, the forest giving way to the fields that marked the official castle grounds, Robert reached over for Lorelai's hand. She gave it, and he squeezed lightly, rubbing his thumb along hers. It felt natural, not forced in the least. Most of all, it felt good.

They rode up to the castle on the horses, Ginny and Noelle asleep in their adult riders' laps. Patricia met them at the door with one of her staff, and together, they carted the girls off to their rooms to rest, though not before Patricia ordered Robert to enjoy himself, to not dare come home before dark. It was hard for Robert to watch his daughter go without him, but a whisper of a thrill coursed through him now that he and Lorelai were alone.

"I'll help you with the horses," Robert told Lorelai. She nodded and nudged Billie Jean toward the stables, Robert and Dexter on their heels.

Fifteen minutes later, flakes of hay in their stalls and tack cleaned and hung up, the horses were put away. Lorelai was bent over the barn sink, a small black kitten at her heels. Her snug jeans complemented not just the heart-shaped backside he couldn't keep his eyes off, but shapely, strong legs as well. He recalled the short, black dress she'd worn that showcased them and felt himself swell behind his own jeans.

Before he could put too much thought into it, his hands were on her waist, and he was spinning her around to face him.

Her deep-green eyes met his gaze, drawing him in like a tractor beam. Then his lips were on hers, and he was back to seeing nothing, feeling nothing but the woman in front of him.

His tongue parted her lips, teasing out hers to meet him. When he nibbled on her bottom lip, she moaned into his mouth, and he was a goner. His hands found the back of her neck, and he pulled her against him.

Robert released her hair from its tie so that it tumbled down her back. Burying his nose in her auburn curls, inhaling deeply, Robert was treated to the scent of his early adulthood. His father and mother both gone, his need to become King imminent and pressing. He'd learned to ride then, had become quite good at it.

The chestnut woodchips, the earthy hay, even the pungent manure, all served to bring him back to that loss. He cried out a small sob against Lorelai's lips. She seemed to understand—of course, she would, since this place housed her painful memories as well—and covered his mouth, his ache with her own. Her tongue glided across his lip while her arms wrapped around his neck. She hoisted herself up onto his hips, her legs cinched around him, holding herself up.

He cupped his hands under her butt, devouring her as he walked them over to the bales of unflaked hay. Setting her down gently, he bent down over her, pulling back from the kiss to gaze over her. Her hair now wild, she looked as untamed as he knew her to be. She was irresistible.

"What are you looking at?" she whispered. Her voice was thick as the air in early Spring, sensual and lazy with lust. Good God, this woman would be his undoing.

"I can't believe I didn't notice you before, Lorelai. You're perfect. Stunning."

"I don't know how you didn't notice me. I was so enamored with you."

He leaned back to look her in the eyes. "You really liked me? I thought your brother was just giving me a hard time when we were kids."

She scowled up at him, but her eyes danced. God, she was beautiful.

"Don't be obtuse—of course, I liked you. I actually more than liked you. You didn't see me hanging on your every word? Practically drooling over you?"

"Wasn't I a bit old for you?" he teased.

She stuck her tongue out at him, and before she could retract it, he closed his mouth over hers, drawing her tongue back out to tangle with his. She tasted like fruit, sweet and ripe. He trailed his fingers along her jawline before she took them and moved her mouth over them, sucking and drawing her tongue along the tips.

A growl emanated from his chest, and he had no more control of his faculties after that. In a frenzy of hands and mouths, Robert tore at Lorelai's clothing, while she did her best from her position of submission to rid him of his chambray button-down. His lips traced her neck down until he got to a white lace bra that stopped him in his tracks. His growl turned into a feral cry for more, and he reached around her back, unclasping the thin lace.

Perfect, perked breasts tumbled into his willing hands,

nipples hard and pink. He enveloped them with his lips, teased her buds with his tongue until her cry of pleasure matched his own desire. Robert sucked as much of the soft flesh into his mouth as he could, delighted to find more of it than he knew what to do with at that moment. He'd learn, by God, if it took him a lifetime. He'd study her until he knew how to please each inch of her edible body.

Lorelai's head was tossed back, her spine arched so that her pelvis ground into his, her mouth parted. He was more than half hard at this point. He'd never been filled with so much need before. Sure, he'd been attracted to Marjorie— that was never the problem in their relationship. But the more he touched Lorelai, tasted her on his lips, the more the desire grew. He wasn't sure, as her hands worked over his now-bare chest and dipped below his jeans to tease the tip of him, he could ever sate that aching want for her. That scared and electrified him to the core.

"Help me with this infernal buckle," Lorelai begged, smiling up at him. He nodded.

He'd do anything she asked. Anything.

He fumbled with his riding buckle, a complicated contraption that made him want to slap the version of himself who'd dressed that morning. When Lorelai's head rose and her lips found his neck, his earlobe, he gave up. Instead, he focused on her simpler, classier belt, loosing it immediately. Her pants followed, and then, like he'd unwrapped a present designed solely for his own tastes, she was there before him in nothing but thin, white-laced underwear that left nothing to the imagination.

"Jesus, Lorelai," he grumbled. "You're, you're…" he started, unable to find the words to match the beauty beneath him. Instead, he shook his head and smiled, knowing just what to do to show her how he felt without saying a word.

"Come here. I want you, Lorelai." He held out her hand for her to take, and when she did, the fire that had started in his chest migrated to their tenuous union of fingers and skin. When he pulled her close so that her bare breasts were pressed against him, that fire spread to each cell touched by one of hers. She branded him with her passion, left him knowing he'd never be the same if he made love to her as he was planning. He also realized, like a chump, he'd gotten her all riled up without a condom to follow through.

She must have seen the brief hesitation in his eyes because she pulled back, covered her chest with her arm.

"We don't have to," she cautioned. In hearing her voice, in the choice she gave him, he broke, knowing he was already claimed by her, no matter what happened next. He swept her back into his arms and bent down to kiss her.

"I want to. I need to. I just don't have…"

She shook her head, her smile knowing.

"It's okay. I'm on birth control."

"Are you sure? You should know I haven't been with anyone since Ginny's mother."

She nodded against him, and he took it as all the invitation he needed. She was a goddess. A naked, feral goddess. And so he set upon worshipping her.

Half an hour later, he lay down next to her, pulling her to his chest, which rose and fell like he'd run a marathon. God, if only all exercise was as satisfying. When he put his nose to her hair and inhaled, he smelled the pine from the forest, along with something sweeter, something more feminine. She was intoxicating as hell, and for a second, when he felt himself swell with desire again, he considered climbing back on top of her for round two, but the other muscles in his body cried out in mutiny.

How on earth was he ever supposed to get enough of this woman?

"That was—" she began, her breath hot on his chest. She finished her thought with her lips pressed lightly to his chest.

"I know. It was." She didn't need to explain what had just happened. He'd felt it, too. In fact, he was still working through how to cope with his feelings about the love they'd made when she pushed his shoulder back to the hay, which was softer than he'd originally thought. Then, to his utter surprise and delight, she climbed on top of him again.

He shivered with pleasure, still sensitive from their first go around.

"You're going to be the death of me, woman."

Lorelai beamed down at him as her hips rocked back and forth. He marveled at how she fit even better this way—especially when he'd have considered her perfect for him the first time. When he imagined all they had to explore about each other, his chest constricted with emotion he'd been keeping at bay.

"Oh, but what a way to go," she said before lowering her breasts to his chest and riding him into the evening.

KRISTINE LYNN

CHAPTER SEVEN: THE COURTING

When Lorelai opened her eyes, the sky held just a hint of the disappearing day along its western horizon. The fading black into deep blue looked like a painting she'd seen in the Museum of Modern Art when she'd lived in New York. Mixed with the nutty undertones of the Oriental Beech and other barn smells that swirled around her, not to mention the naked man to her side, the moment confused her senses with memories from across her recent and distant past.

As she inhaled the unique aroma of cinnamon musk on the skin of Robert's chest, she couldn't help but wonder if what she was experiencing wasn't her future as well.

He moved beneath her, and when his eyes opened slowly and he took in his surroundings, she ran a hand through his hair and kissed the soft skin of his exposed shoulder. His eyes were such a deep blue. Not cerulean, like the sea, like his brother's, nor like the twilight that engulfed them, but like the sky on a bright, cloudless day. They were the blue of his country's land, its flag, its national flower. He was made to be the king of this illustrious country, she could see that in every cell of his body. She couldn't help but feel she was as much made for him, though, and wondered how that would work with his duties as a father, a king.

"I'd say 'Good morning,' but it looks like that isn't the case. What time is it?"

"Around six in the evening. Are you comfortable?"

The hay wasn't the worst place to have made a temporary bed—it would hold in the heat and was softer than the ground, but that didn't mean it was what he was used to. She guessed his California King feather bed was more suited to his tastes.

"I wouldn't leave this moment if I didn't think we'd have the whole national guard descending upon us in the morning."

Heat spread through her cheeks at the sentiment, then moved south when he crooked his head up to catch her lips in his.

"I had a good time this afternoon," she admitted. That was a horrific understatement, but until she knew if this was more than a one-night joining of two bodies who'd been hurtling through space, destined to crash into one another, she didn't want to betray too much. She still loved him, always would, but in light of having slept together just once—well, twice, actually—that seemed woefully out of place.

"Me, too." This time, he kissed her shoulder, but the result was the same. God, how she still wanted him. If anything, the previous few hours had increased the wanting, not lessened it. "What changed your mind about having dinner with me?" he asked.

"Oh, is that what we're calling it now?" she teased, her bare chest pressed against his, her breathing finally regulated from the exertion of the best sex in her life and the nerves of waking up next to her teenage crush. Her hand tucked a stray curl behind his ear, unable to stop seeking out ways to touch him.

"Well, I was ravenous, I'll give you that," he tossed back, a half-smile she now recognized as playful turning up a corner of his lips. "But you still didn't answer my question."

She grew serious, recalling the exact moment she'd decided to give in to the "dinner", aka the love that had never really dissipated for this man. The image of watching him ride, his niece in his lap, his daughter in hers, was branded in her memory forever. She'd felt like she had a family again, one she'd conjured up on all her darkest nights in New York.

"It was riding with you, your girls this morning. You aren't the same man who didn't notice me when we were younger. The same man who threw away women. I see that now." She prayed she was right.

"I can't believe I ever was that man. I'm so sorry, Lor—" he started, but then her lips found his and she was lost in him again as his mouth parted to let her in.

"Shhh," she whispered into him. "No apologies. We started over. That's enough for me."

And it was, oh, how it was.

"Can I take you to dinner, actual dinner now so we can talk? I have so much I want to ask you."

Her heart skipped a beat. A date somehow sounded scarier than lying naked with the man she'd loved her whole life.

"I can do you one better," she told him. "Why don't I cook so we aren't interrupted by gawkers?"

He smiled, the gesture wrinkling the skin around his eyes. It was sexy as hell. As was the small patch of peppered gray in the hair around his temples. He'd grown up while she was away, but then again, so had she.

"I'd like that. You're not a vegetarian or anything silly like that, are you?"

She laughed, enjoying the light banter between them.

"Not a chance. New York made the best damn steak I've ever eaten, so that pretty much solidified my diet."

"Well, then. Let the gauntlet be thrown down. You can cook tonight, but I've got tomorrow night up on my turf.

I'll grill you a slab of meat so good you'll forget you ever tasted one before it."

She laughed again, but the exuberance died away in her chest when she realized he'd just set up two dates back-to-back with her. She'd already fallen back head-over-boots for him, so she didn't know what she'd do if he spurned her after drawing her in closer still. Oh, well. She'd never run from a challenge before, and she wasn't about to start borrowing trouble now.

Lorelai pressed up on her arm, realizing how kinked her muscles were from lying on the hay.

"Wait. Let me help you up." Robert hopped up effortlessly, and Lorelai tried not to gawk as his full, naked form stretched over her. He was a Greek god, cut from stone, chiseled to perfection. When he offered his hand, she took it, noticing how his gaze trailed her body in the same appreciative way. Was it actually possible he felt the same about her?

God, how she wanted to believe it, but history hadn't favored her where he was concerned.

They dressed quickly, Robert helping her with the clasps on her bra, a more intimate gesture than it had been when he'd taken it off her body. Before she knew it, they were on the stairs up to her apartment, a mere four hours after they'd left the girls at the castle with Patricia. It seemed years had passed, rather than minutes.

Lorelai opened the door, nervous about inviting Robert inside. Sure, he'd been there before, but he'd shown up as King, not her lover.

Lover. She hoped the conversation wouldn't stray to her experience on that topic. Having borne witness to his "experience" from her vantage point of living above the barn where most of his trysts occurred, hers was woefully inadequate by comparison. She'd been with one man—the only man who'd tried and failed to love her more than the ghost he competed against. In the end, she'd broken his heart and spirit. It was one of her greatest regrets, not opening herself up to him.

It was as if she knew Robert would enter her life again, that this chance for them, though over a decade in the making, wasn't over yet.

"It's beautiful, Lor. You've made it a home."

She beamed, watching him wander through her small, private space.

He picked up the small, wooden carving of a horse.

"Your father's?" he asked. She nodded. He'd carved it for her when she'd gone to New York for school. A reminder of what awaited her when she returned.

"How did you know?"

"I have one from him. A gift for helping out his stock of horses when we had a bad winter the one before he… Before he passed."

Robert set down the horse and was at Lorelai's side before the first tear fell. He caught it with his thumb, caressed her cheek with his hand.

"I miss him."

"I know you do. Believe me, I get it. My folks were nothing like your dad, but still, when they're gone, that doesn't seem to matter, does it?"

Of course, he would understand her loss. He'd traversed the same rocky terrain with his brother, like she had with hers.

"No, it doesn't. And your parents were wonderful. They were so kind to my father and me. To Gregory when he wasn't wreaking havoc on their property."

They both chuckled at the memories of Gregory and Prince Philip's shenanigans as teens. More than a discreet media payoff had occurred to keep their names from the press.

"They were pretty good when it came to that. But your dad," he started. Lorelai caught the way his voice cracked, his eyes watered. "Your dad is who I measure my own parenting against."

There was no stopping the stray tears that crested over

her bottom lid at this admission. Robert was a single father like hers had been most of his life. She recalled the loneliness etched on her father's face when she'd get up at night for a glass of water and he would be sipping a drink, alone, gazing out the dark window at a future he'd never see.

Her heart ached for him. What she wouldn't give to show him what she'd accomplished since he'd passed. It also ached for Robert, who had sacrificed greatly for his own daughter. Ginny would appreciate it one day, but that didn't mean Lorelai wanted Robert to suffer until then. He deserved some help, and maybe, just maybe, she could put aside her own misgivings about being a maternal figure and at least help Robert care for Ginny. As long as she still carved out time to train for taking over the hunt. That was what she was there for, after all.

"So, um, on a lighter note, what're you cooking us?"

Lorelai opened her small fridge, procuring some butter and capers, then remembering she had asparagus in the lower drawer, grabbed the bunch as well.

"Just a simple pasta with a white wine and butter sauce. Some veggies. Nothing fancy."

Robert's hands found her hips while she was bent over, and his hand ran up along her spine until it found the nape of her neck. His caress was both halting and invigorating at the same time. She wanted nothing more than to drop the food to the counter and feast on other, more pressing desires. Her stomach growled, however, threatening mutiny if she didn't at least attempt to sate its needs.

"I don't know how I am ever supposed to get enough of you," he purred into her back. Reaching his hands around her waist, he squeezed her breasts, which were full and heavy with desire. Though, it was his words that called to her more than his touch; not that she minded the latter in the least.

She'd waited so long for this man to notice her in the way she had him, and when she'd thought it impossible, that their time had passed with the changing seasons, she'd been proved wrong. He was there, in her apartment, whispering sweet nothings to her. It was all she could do to convince herself this wasn't a dream, that it was real.

More than that, she tried hard not to worry it would fade when his appetite for her abated.

"The first, and most important thing you need to know about me is that if I get hungry, I'm a bear that isn't much fun to be around. Many a person has come close to losing a limb because it looked suspiciously close to a turkey leg while I was starving."

Robert laughed, stepped back, and let his hands fall. "Okay, okay. I know when I've been bested. But don't think I'm not ravishing you as soon as you've got some food in that fine belly of yours. We wouldn't want you mistaking parts of my anatomy for bratwurst or anything."

She smiled, put the food on the counter, and reached up on her toes to kiss Robert.

"Bratwurst, huh? You don't think you're being a little too generous there? Summer sausage, maybe?" She giggled, but when mischief danced in his eyes and his hands twitched, she squealed and ran out of the kitchen.

"Oh, you've crossed a line, little lady." When he caught her around the corner to her bedroom, he tossed her on the bed and tickled her sides until she cried out. Tears from laughing so hard streamed down her cheeks, dampening her blouse.

"Mercy!" she hollered. "Please. Oh, God, I'm so ticklish. Pleeeease." Her stomach cramped from laughing.

"I think you owe an apology to the little prince before I think of letting up."

She couldn't control the fit of giggles that sprung from her chest at the moniker he'd assigned his member.

"The… little… prince?" she got out between gasps and convulsions of laughter.

"Oh, now you're in for it," he said, moving down to tickle her feet. Halfway down, he stopped at her abdomen and, lifting her shirt, pressed his lips to the spot where her stomach met her hip.

All the laughter died in her chest in an instant, and the fire that had raged within her earlier grew, consuming her hunger, her good sense.

A sound not unlike a purr came from her throat, unbidden.

Robert moved his mouth to the top of her jeans again and traced his tongue along the edge. The purr became a soft growl. There was no way she could ever get enough of him, either.

"You're not too hungry, are you?" he asked. His fingers expertly undid the buttons to her jeans and pulled them down to just above her knees, trapping her in a jail of pure lust.

The last thought she had before she blacked out in her third orgasm of the evening was that this man would be the death of her, but the exquisite joy in that demise would be worth it. Oh, so worth it.

Sometime later that night, Lorelai heard a knock on her door. She only vaguely registered Robert shifting beside her, the soft padding of his feet on her wood floors, and the distant sound of him talking to someone.

She was far too hungry, too tired, too physically depleted to piece together more than that, but when the aroma of melted cheese, tomato sauce, and garlic wafted over her, her senses came back to life and she sprang from the mattress like it was in flames.

The first article of clothing she came across was Robert's chambray shirt, so she stuffed her arms through the sleeves, buttoning it up as she walked. She didn't even bother with underwear at that point. Her stomach was in full-fledged mutiny, roaring with how unfairly it had been treated all day.

Robert whistled as she walked out of the bedroom.

"If you want half a chance to eat tonight, I'd suggest a pair of baggy sweatpants and an extra-large shirt. You're entirely too sexy in that get-up." He walked over to her and slid his hands up the fabric of his own shirt. "No panties? Jesus, what are you trying to do to me, Lor?"

All she had to offer in reply was a weak smile. Her body was betraying her ability to stand, to talk. She couldn't recall a time she'd been more ravenous.

"Let's get you fed, huh? Can you steer me toward the plates?"

Lorelai pointed to the cabinet behind them, then sat at her modest dining table. Her father had made it, and along with the small wooden horse Robert had discovered earlier, it was her most treasured possession.

"What is this?" she asked, gesturing toward the table. Two boxes of pizza were laid before her, even a bottle of ranch to accompany them. Not once in Aldonia had she had pizza growing up. Sure, her birth country had its own savory delights that she'd missed, but the sight of her favorite New York comfort food in the home she'd been raised in was enough to bring tears to her eyes.

"Pizza. I heard it was one of your favorites."

"Who—" she began, but stopped herself. *Gregory.* "But how did you get it here?" To her knowledge, there wasn't a pizzeria anywhere within five hundred miles.

"Patricia made it. I had the ingredients flown in from New York."

"When did you do that?" she asked.

"Last week. I was hoping to keep it a surprise until I could cook for you up at the castle, but reinforcements were needed if I'm to take advantage of you in my shirt." He winked at her, and her stomach rumbled a reply that she'd better ignore the heat building in her chest and satisfy it. Or else. Robert chuckled. "Let's eat."

Lorelai couldn't contain the surprise that spread across her face at his touching gesture. He'd flown in ingredients to her favorite food and had it cooked and delivered to her doorstep in true New York fashion. And all of this he'd planned before she'd slept with him. It dawned on her, then, that it was after midnight.

"Patricia made this for you, for *me* in the middle of the night?"

"Yeah, I owe her big time, but for the time being, I gave her the rest of the weekend off starting tomorrow morning, so I may have to head back early to take care of the girls. Now, eat."

Lorelai didn't need to be told again. She dove into the first box and almost bawled when she saw the meat lover's pizza stretched before her. It was heaven in a box.

She slid two slices on her plate and, folding the slice in half like a taco, she went to work on the much-needed sustenance despite the still-too-warm cheese that scorched the roof of her mouth with the first bite. Halfway through the slice, she slowed and took a minute to appreciate the flavor. It was almost exactly like the pizza from her favorite hole-in-the-wall joint in New York. How had Robert pulled this off? More importantly, *why*?

There was no way she was ruining a perfectly great pizza with dreary questions though, so she stayed silent until the rumbling in her stomach abated.

"I'll come help you tomorrow. I can afford some time off from here if you need me to stay up there a few days until Aurelia gets back with Philip."

Robert got up from his chair, his food half eaten, and walked over to her. He tipped her chin up to meet his and gave her a kiss so soft, she wasn't sure he'd been there at all, if it weren't for her flushed cheeks and dampness between her legs that argued otherwise.

"You're amazing, Lor. Are you sure you can get away?"

"I am. The staff has been trained and they all seem good. Better than good, actually."

"Okay. But only on one condition."

Lorelai threw him a wayward glance.

"What's that?"

He kissed her again, and this time, his mouth opened and the heat of his tongue melted her lips, teasing her open for him. She obliged, and when their tongues met, the warmth on her skin spread through her limbs. Would she ever tire of wanting this man now that she had him?

Robert pulled back, his forehead still leaning against hers.

"You stay with me, in my quarters."

That wasn't such a tough sell, but Lorelai didn't want to seem too eager, even though that had been her dream since she was a girl—be with Robert. Like, really be with him. Live beside him as his partner.

There was a second part to that dream, but it was much too soon to breathe it to life by thinking about it.

"I think I can manage that. But I don't want Ginny to know we're together. Or sleeping together. Or whatever this is."

Great. Real smooth, Lorelai.

Robert smiled down at her.

"I wouldn't mind her thinking we're together. But I promise I'll be on my best behavior when we're around the girls. At night, though…" With that, he dove into her neck, nibbling it like she'd been doing with her pizza. Her food left in front of her, she leaned back against the table, letting Robert have his way with her again. There would be time to eat, and if they wanted to enjoy pizza the true New York way, some of it would have to be eaten cold.

With that, she wrapped her arms around Robert's shoulders, sating her one true hunger, the only desire strong enough to risk everything she'd built for herself.

Him. Robert. Her muse and undoing wrapped in one delicious package.

CHAPTER EIGHT: THE JOB

Robert peeked his head around the corner and held his breath. Lorelai sat on the plush carpet, her long legs tucked underneath her, Ginny curled up like a kitten in her lap. Though he could sense Lorelai's hesitation when Ginny had first thrown herself into her arms two weeks prior, the two now got along like they'd been together since Ginny's birth. One of the newer and less informed staff had mistaken the pair for mother and daughter, to Ginny's delight. She'd bragged about it for two days.

To see them sitting together, Lorelai reading *Harry Potter* to his four-year-old, he might even make that mistake. Lorelai's voice rang across the threshold of the expansive living room, thick with a booming, faux British accent when she read Dumbledore's part. The affectation caused a fit of giggles from Ginny and a warming of Robert's heart, which swelled at the interaction.

Every day, Ginny had grown less and less vocal about wanting a mother, and more and more attached to Lorelai. She wasn't the only one, either. Robert found himself rushing through his royal duties to get back to Lorelai faster. Nothing filled him with more joy than to see Lorelai trotting along the path from the mountains that flanked the east side of the castle, smiling atop her horse, a few hounds by her side at the end of each day. She was a natural on the back of a horse and heck if he didn't find himself enjoying being in the saddle again, thanks to her. He'd even taken to joining her on her morning rides, sometimes with Ginny, but many times alone.

When they would head out without his daughter, they'd ride to the field where they'd gone on their first ride and make love on the grass. With the likelihood that Ginny would barge into their bedroom in the middle of the night, or when she first woke up, the field had become their sanctuary—the only place they could be themselves and relish in their newfound love.

He was certain at this point that the previously forbidden four-letter word was the emotion brewing inside him, threatening to spill over. That didn't mean he could say anything out loud just yet. It was too soon according to Philip and Gregory. Not that he trusted the latter with anything resembling his love life.

Lorelai had been with them two weeks already and hadn't indicated that she was heading back home in the near future, so that had to count for something. She'd only suggested it once, when Philip and Aurelia had returned, and he'd told her he wanted her to stay as long as she liked. That she hadn't packed up and sprinted back to her apartment over the barn was a constant source of joy and contentment for Robert. Heck, she even looked the part, accepting the clothes and jewelry befitting a woman dating the King he bestowed upon her with no regard for cost.

She was still his Lorelai, through and through, just as comfortable in her riding jeans and cotton button-down, but damn if she didn't look as if she belonged there, too, in the roles of Queen and Ginny's mother.

Which was why he was bound and determined to do everything in his power to keep her happy, keep her there with him.

Each morning, he woke before her and made sure he

had an assortment of bagels—New York bagels, of course—and coffee for her to choose from. Each evening, he presented her with a bouquet of flowers from the royal garden, a note telling her how pleased he was to have her in his life again attached to the stems. When his duties didn't pull him away, he spoiled her with day trips to the Black Sea, to his family's property on the coast, and expensive dinners where he would ply her with wine before taking her back to the castle to ravish her senseless.

He just couldn't get enough of her.

He'd even been planning a trip for just the two of them later in the month where, if things kept up like they were going until then, he would ask to be his wife, Ginny's mom. Except watching them now, how the heck would he be able to wait that long? He had a complete family—a woman he couldn't get enough of, and a mother for his daughter. It was all his lonely nights spent awake praying come to fruition.

He just didn't want to rush Lorelai, who had barely become comfortable alone with Ginny. If she loved him back, it came with all the love, money, and travel she could desire. But it meant responsibility, too—being a mother to Ginny, a partner to the crown. It was a lot; he understood what he asked of her. What he didn't know was whether or not it was too much.

Oh, well. He was happy as a hound with a bone right now, and that was enough for him. The rest would fall into place at the right time. Or it wouldn't. No use fussing over it when he couldn't control her end of the outcome he desired.

He finished off the turkey sandwiches he'd made with a few of the ripe strawberries from the garden on the side and carried all three plates over to his girls, a surprise tucked away in his breast pocket for Lorelai.

"Daddy, listen to Lory-lai. She does a better Dumbledore than you." Ginny giggled, eliciting a smile from both him and Lorelai.

"Does she now? Well, this I have to see." He set the plates down, but just as he was about to dive headfirst into his lunch, a faint meowing emanated from behind the sitting room wall. Lorelai must have noticed it, too, because her head jerked toward the sound. Only Ginny looked nonplussed, the green end of the fruit hanging from her lips.

"Ginny," Robert said as calmly as he could. "Why does it sound like there is a cat behind our wall?"

Ginny stopped chewing and smiled, green and red teeth making her look like a deranged Christmas elf.

"I dunno," she said, but her gaze dropped to the floor—a telltale sign she was up to mischief of one kind or another.

Lorelai stood Ginny up and walked with Robert toward the sound that grew more insistent now. He glanced at Lorelai, and she met his gaze with humor and understanding, a wink thrown in at the last minute. He winked back and threw open the door to Ginny's room to see a flash of black dart out across his feet and straight into the lap of his guilty-as-sin daughter.

Lorelai coughed back a laugh while he struggled to keep his lips pursed in feigned frustration. The "cat" was actually no more than a fresh newborn kitten nuzzled up against Ginny's stomach, purring away like it missed its mother. The look Ginny gave it back was one of pure, unadulterated maternal love. Robert didn't miss the same look on Lorelai's face as she gazed down over the situation.

Maybe it isn't too soon, after all.

"Ginny," he said, trying to make his voice firm, to keep the chortle that threatened to escape at bay, "how did this kitten come to find itself in your room? Or in the castle at all?" He put his hands on his hips for added emphasis, but it did nothing to tamper his daughter's spirit.

"This is Hannah," she told him, holding up the kitten from under its arms. "I just looooove her. Isn't she so cute?" That last word sounded like an opera singer belted out a high C.

He needed to reevaluate his strategy, and quickly before his daughter got the best of him.

"Well, hi there, Hannah." He reached down to pet the infant feline, considering the surge of affection for the animal growing in his chest a moral failing of some sort. He had a no-animals-in-the-house rule, that it seemed had gone to the birds. "She is cute, Ginny, but why is she in your room?"

"'Cause I don't want her to be stepped on. She's so tiny the horses wouldn't see her, and she's my favorite of the new kitties so I gotta protect her." She nuzzled the cat with her cheek, evoking the softest feral cry Robert had ever heard.

"How long has she been there, honey?"

"Just since Uncle Philip got home." *A week.* The cat had been living in that room for a week. How was it still alive? How could he call himself a diligent father, a king even, if he couldn't rein in a four-year-old?

"Um, what are you feeding it, honey?" Lorelai asked.

Good question, he mouthed over Ginny's head. Lorelai winked again, somehow keeping the smile off her face in what must be a Herculean effort of will.

"I bring it milk from my cereal, and some of my chicken and fish when it's bedtime." The child turned back to him. "I watched Lory-lai feed the kitties in the barn. I'm not stupid, Daddy."

"I don't think you are, Ginny, but…"

Just as Robert was about to lay down the law, tell his daughter that despite being scared the cat would get hurt, it was an outside animal and she could visit it there, Lorelai stepped in. Thank God, too, because he didn't think he could bite down on his lip any harder without drawing blood. His smile almost cracked through and then all would be lost.

"Robert, could I talk to you over here?"

He nodded, needing a break to figure out how to handle the fact that his daughter had managed to sneak a live animal into the castle under the nose of his guards, Patricia, and her staff, as well as he and his family, including Lorelai.

Once they were out of hearing range of Ginny, Lorelai bit her bottom lip, her gaze pinned to the ground. If he didn't know any better, he'd say she looked just as guilty as the cat-rescuer in the other room.

"This whole thing is my fault, I'm afraid."

"Did you sneak the cat in for her?" he asked, only half kidding. It would be the only plausible way the adults would have missed it living in Ginny's bedroom for a week.

The look she shot him said he'd better be one hundred percent joking if he wanted to live to talk about it. He threw his hands up in defeat. He was getting royally steamrolled by the two women he loved most in this world, and neither of them seemed very sympathetic to the fact that it made him look weak. Unfit to rule.

"Fine. Then why is it your fault?" His hands were back on his hips, but Lorelai tucked her hands around his waist, drawing him in, lowering his defensive wall.

"Because she must have overheard me talking to the stable staff about the barn kittens. There's a new batch barely two weeks old, and I informed the staff only half would make it because of the cold that's come in, as well as going under foot of one of the half-ton animals loafing about. I had no idea she was there, I promise."

Robert's resolve dissipated with the light, fall breeze that blew in the open window. How could he deny this woman anything, including his faith in her? He was falling for her by the minute, that was for certain.

"So, what do you suggest we do about the kitten?" he asked, though when he saw Lorelai's eyebrows rise, her cheeks and eyes brighten in front of him, he wished he'd kept the question to himself.

"Well…" she started.

"Besides keep it. That's a nonstarter for me."

"Why?" she asked. This time, it was her hands on her hips, one jutting out, calling attention to the form-fitting jeans she wore. When his pants tightened in the telltale way they did whenever she was around, he silently cursed the woman for being far more effective with the gesture than he could ever hope to be.

"Well, I don't like animals in the house. They're dirty, they go to the bathroom wherever they darn well please, and they bring in other critters I like even less."

"Wow. That's a rather limited view, don't you think?"

"Well, where do you think the kitten has been going to the bathroom for the past week?"

The smile fell from her face and a case of righteous indignation swelled his chest, thankfully letting the steam fall from the other parts of him that were solely interested in the perfect, round backside that spun toward Ginny's room, swaying as she hurried to answer that question herself.

"Ginny?" Lorelai called out. "Can you come here a minute? You, too, Robert."

His chest deflated with the tone of her voice. He made his way to the bedroom, only to find Lorelai holding a small box with what looked like shavings at the bottom of it. What the—?

"What is this, hun?" Lorelai asked, far more coherent than he was at the moment.

"That's the kitty's bathroom," Ginny replied, no hint of irony in her voice. "I made it like the one the momma has in your barn and when that stuff gets wet, I just 'place it."

Robert choked back a laugh.

"Where do you get the shavings?" Lorelai pressed. Robert noticed the laugh Lorelai was trying—and failing—to contain in her chest by the quivering in her lower jaw. It was as adorable as Ginny was in her subterfuge. As infuriating as well.

"From the barn. I sneak 'em in my backpack." Ginny giggled, and Robert couldn't keep his smile from spreading like wildfire across his face.

"That's real smart, Ginny. Isn't it, Robert?"

Robert nodded, stunned silent by this interesting turn of events. His daughter had been taking care of a feral animal in her suite for a week and no one—not even one of the adults—was the wiser. Jesus, she'd even figured out how to care for the thing properly. He wanted to be mad at the sneaking around that had occurred behind his back, but frankly, he was impressed. The kid was only four years old, for Christ's sake.

"It is, honey. I'm just a little sad you felt like you had to hide it from Lorelai and me."

"Yeah, but you said no animals, so I was 'fraid you wouldn't let me keep Hannah. And oooh, I want to keep her so bad, Daddy. Look at her. She's a good girl."

The darned thing was curled up against Ginny's chest, leaving him as defenseless as the poor kitten would have been in the barn. But it was Lorelai's protective arm wrapped around his daughter that left him completely exposed, vulnerable.

"She's pretty great," he murmured, his sight set on Lorelai.

"Can we keep her?" Ginny asked.

Robert shook the thoughts of the woman he'd grown to love from his head and focused on his daughter and the kitten she was discussing.

"Um, well," he started. When he glanced at Lorelai, though, darn if the last of his argument for why she certainly could not keep a cat in her bedroom flew the coop. Her pleading eyes bored into his chest, nestling beside his heart. "I, um, I guess that would be okay."

Ginny squealed, and even Lorelai let out a small gasp and giggle at the news. The smiles on both their faces and the way they embraced each other while they jumped in a congratulatory circle reinforced his decision. Heck, he'd let in a whole brood of cats if it meant seeing his two ladies that happy. Not that he'd ever let them know that, of course.

Ginny ran back to her room with the kitten, talking the poor thing's ear off about how happy they were going to be together, forever. When they were alone, Lorelai wrapped her arms around Robert, pulling him close. He inhaled her scent—floral and wholly feminine— appreciating how she was changing him, day by day.

He was working less, spending more time with his daughter. He'd even begun to love riding, something he'd never been able to admit in his thirty-eight years. The greatest gift she'd bestowed upon him, though, was opening his heart again. He didn't think he'd ever get another chance at love after Marjorie had left him, nor did he feel he deserved it. But Lorelai showed him why he did, and that it was possible. That was reason enough to love her, not taking into account how amazing she was with his daughter, nor as head of the stables. She fit into his life perfectly. No one was more surprised by this than him.

"Thank you," she breathed into his chest. The warmth from her breath seeped into his skin, traveling down to his abdomen which flared with a heat only she was capable of producing. "You've made her so happy."

"I'd do anything to keep that smile on her face. On yours, too, Lor. You know that, right?"

She nodded against him. "I do."

He cleared his throat. "Speaking of, I wanted to give you something." Even though he could wrap her up in his arms again any time he felt like it, stepping back from her was always like fighting against gravity. He was drawn to her body any time he was near it and ached for it when he wasn't.

"You don't have to give me anything. You've already given me so much."

"Nothing you haven't earned. This is a gift."

"But why?"

"Do I need a reason to spoil the woman I'm seeing?"

It felt too casual, calling her a woman he was seeing. But he wasn't ready to ask her to be more. Not just yet. Soon, though. He felt the pull growing stronger each second he spent with her.

"I guess not."

He procured the small velvet box from his breast pocket and held it out to her.

"What is it?"

"Open it, silly."

When she did, she exhaled a light gasp as her hand flew to her chest. Her eyes glinted with moisture; he'd chosen correctly. She loved it. Now the question was whether she loved him enough to accept.

"It's beautiful, Robert," she whispered, pulling out the pendant, turning around so he could clasp it. It was a diamond-encrusted charm in the shape of a key strung on a white gold chain as delicate as the skin he set it on.

"There's more," he told her, spinning her back to admire the way the necklace fell to just above her perfect cleavage. He'd have to thank the jeweler for his precision where that was concerned.

"There couldn't possibly be."

But she was grinning ear to ear and optimism flooded his chest. This might be it, the second chance he'd always hoped for.

Robert lifted the backing of the box that had held the necklace in place to reveal an actual key.

Her brows pulled together in confusion, and he waited a beat to see if she put the pieces together herself. When she held the metal key out to him and her shoulders shrugged, however, he figured he'd better help her out.

"It's symbolic, really. Especially since the guards are the only ones who grant access to the castle or inside its walls, but I read online that this is something Americans do."

Why wasn't she smiling, running into his arms and shouting that yes, she'd love to live with him?

"When do Americans give someone a key?" But as she said it, understanding registered on her face. "Wait, are you asking me to, to…"

"To move in with me, yes. Will you, Lorelai? Because you fit up here, with me. You can still run the stables from here, but we can hire on more staff to cover the nights you were on call. I've even found a good stable manager who can run things when we travel on state business. What do you say?"

Robert considered himself to be a terrific reader of people, of their expressions, so why the heck couldn't he get a read on Lorelai at that moment? This was everything he thought she wanted. And heck if it hadn't taken a load of courage to even ask her. Now the way she was looking at him made him wonder if he should pour himself three fingers of whiskey before she gave her reply.

She sighed, and he felt the air leave his lungs as well.

"Robert, this is a generous offer, but I'm training to take over the hunt, and as it is, I'm struggling to find time to train the horses and run the dogs. I've loved staying with you and Ginny, and don't get me started on how beautiful your property is, but it's not where I belong. I came here to run the stables, the hunt. How will it look if I bought the stables from you only to hand over the management to someone else?"

Robert was stunned silent for the second time that afternoon, this time not in a way that felt good. It was precisely why he couldn't say anything. Shouldn't. And why he was compelled to. Curse this woman for coming home, for confusing what had been a pretty straightforward and simple life. He'd hired a huntsman already. What he needed was a partner, someone he could trust, come home to, and build a life outside the crown with, a mother to his daughter. He thought he'd found that, but again, he wasn't enough. He was never going to be enough, was he?

The words were out of his mouth before he could stop

them.

"Simon has the hunt, Lorelai. Jesus, I didn't even know you wanted it. And you'd still own the barn, but does that mean you have to oversee every little thing? Be reasonable. We're good together."

She stepped back like he slapped her, her hands balled into fists.

"And what did you think I wanted? To just sit up here and play house? Wait around to be your wife? Travel around the country in a fancy dress, waving and curtsying behind you? You still don't know me at all, do you, Robert? I'm not Marjorie."

Ouch. That stung. Worse than when he'd found out Marjorie was cheating on him, Lorelai's claim that he didn't know her hurt deep in a place that he was just allowing to break open and be vulnerable again. Sure, he wanted those things she'd spat at him like they were plagues, but he also wanted her to be happy. More than what he thought that should look like.

More than anything.

"Lorelai, I'm sorry," he said. Beyond that, he didn't know what else to offer her. He'd taken away the one thing she'd been trying for without even realizing he did it. Sure, he'd seen her working with the hounds, training them alongside the horses to get them used to each other, but he'd assumed—wrongly, it seemed—that she'd been working with Simon.

"But the hunt is Simon's."

It was posed as a statement, not a question. He nodded.

"I hired him on a three-year contract, Lorelai. I'm sorry. I really am."

"I thought he was provisional." Another statement, but this time, her arms crossed over her chest showed she expected a reply.

"He was. Until last week."

Lorelai shut her eyes and he damn near broke in two

when a rogue tear broke away from between her lids. Maybe she was right, maybe he wasn't paying enough attention.

"And the barn? Why haven't you cashed any of my checks for the property, Robert?"

The color drained from his face. Blood pooled in his lower stomach, curdling and making him sick. He'd wanted the stables to be a wedding gift once he proposed, but would she see it that way?

He opened his mouth to reply and shut it again, something catching his eye, distracting him from winning her back, showing her how wonderful they were together.

A dull orange glow tickled Lorelai's cheek facing the window and then shifted and grew as he watched. What the—?

He whipped his head around to the south-facing window, the one that overlooked Lorelai's apartment, the barn and south stables. He'd loved that window when she first got home so he could watch her work.

Now, though, the view filled him with dread.

She followed his gaze and made her way to the glass, a feral cry erupting from her chest as she watched the south side of her barn consumed in flames.

Oh, my God. How the hell has this happened?

He reached for her, not sure what to do except pull out his phone to dial the emergency number for the fire squad. When he had them on the line, they assured him the crew assigned to watch the castle had seen the blaze and was on their way.

They can still save it. God, he hoped they could save the barn. Or at the very least her apartment. But what of the horses?

Lorelai was off and running before he could touch her, though. Crap. His pulse raced, and his skin erupted in sweat as if he stood in front of the flames. Where was she going? She didn't have the skills to fight this off on her own. She should wait for the crew to come take care of this.

He'd made up his mind before his conscience could stop him.

He took off after her, cursing her for not letting the professionals take care of the fire, cursing himself for being unable to let her go. As he ran down the path after her, the panicked neighing of the horses registered louder than the persistent *thump-thump* of his racing heart and he finally understood.

She was going to set them free.

By running right into the blaze.

He pushed his legs, lungs, heart to go faster, to catch her before she got hurt, or worse. The heat scorched his cheeks when he got close to the stables. Inside must be an inferno. That was what worried him most, especially since he couldn't clap eyes on Lorelai. Where was she? His heart pounded against his chest, a rapid-fire staccato that belied the worry he felt.

What if he was too late? His heart roared with fear.

No. He couldn't think that, not yet.

The only thing he could offer to dispel the rising panic in his chest was his help. He released the barrel locks on the two stalls closest to the north exit of the barn and hollered at the horses inside to run. They took off, instinct winning over. If only Lorelai had been as smart.

"Lorelai," he called out over the roar of the fire that got closer to where he was standing. "Lorelai, let's go!"

He didn't hear anything except the crackling, surging of the flames as they raced toward him. He counted them lucky he couldn't see any other horses in the stalls, any movement at all, but when he heard a thump above him, all that went to hell.

She was in her apartment.

Of course. The table, the horse.

The last two things she owned from her father.

He tore off after her, taking the steps three at a time. When he opened the door, he was met with a wide-eyed, wild-haired Lorelai, tears streaming down her face.

"Please," she pleaded with him. She was dragging the heavy oak table across the floor as smoke circled in around them. The flames wouldn't be far behind. He fought the urge to grab her, hoist her over his shoulder, drag her from the apartment, but her eyes… Her eyes spoke of so much pain, so much loss, that dammit, of course, he would help her.

"We have to hurry."

She nodded and he grabbed the side opposite her, pulling it toward the door. Good God, the table was heavy. There was no way they would be able to drag it further than the edge of the kitchen, and even then, how would they get it outside? He was about to call it quits, go caveman on Lorelai to get her to safety when he heard two sets of footsteps coming up the stairs.

"Robert? Jesus. What are you doing up here? Lorelai? Guys, get out of here—the fire squad is downstairs and they told me the structure doesn't have more than ten minutes left."

Robert glanced at Philip, at Gregory behind him and pointed to the table, his eyes pleading. He'd never been so happy to see his kid brother.

"Then you'd better help us because we aren't leaving without it."

Lorelai let out a choked sob. "Thank you. I'm so sorry."

"We've got this, Lorelai. Grab the horse and the photo."

She nodded and ran to her small bedroom in the back, the tears abated. For now. He knew all of her defenses, all of her insecurities, all of her fears would come running for her the second she paused and assessed the damage, which was extensive from what Robert could tell.

"How'd you find us?" Robert asked the two guys when Lorelai was out of earshot.

"The guard got the call, and when we couldn't find you

in the suite, we looked out and saw you sprinting toward the flames. Not sure that's the smartest move you could've made, big brother."

"No, it wasn't. But I couldn't let her come down alone."

"I get it, but you're not just her … boyfriend, or whatever it is you two are doing. You're the king, and you've got to remember that before you launch headlong into a burning building. Your country needs you."

Robert understood his brother's admonition, heck, he'd even given his brother not-so-dissimilar advice at one point early on in his relationship with Aurelia. But the underlying truth was that, king or not, he needed Lorelai to be any kind of ruler at all. That admission left him reeling, and it would be his own wreckage to sift through when this was all behind them.

When the table was at the door, Robert heaved his side up so that it stood on its end. Crap. It wouldn't fit through. He looked at his brother and friend, a knowing glance shared between them.

"I'll be right back," Gregory shouted over the din and roar. He tore off down the stairs when a thud shook the floor behind Robert. A glance back was all it took to arrest his heart, send him careening back into the smoke-filled room.

Lorelai lay on the ground, her arm extended in front of her, hand still clasped around the frame and small, wooden figurine. He was by her side in a flash, and this time, he didn't need to think twice about slinging her over his shoulder and whisking her away from the danger. Her breath was weak but hot on his back. Thank God she was still breathing.

If anything should happen to her…

"I've got this until Gregory gets back," Philip told him as Robert ran down the steps, Lorelai limp across his shoulders. He met a fire squad corporal at the bottom and handed Lorelai off to him.

"She's everything to me," he told the corporal.

"I understand, Your Grace. I'll take care of her."

Robert nodded, wiped at tears that he hadn't even felt fall on his cheeks. Watching her carted away, lifeless and unresponsive, was more than his heart could take. He needed to save the table for her, needed to give her something after she'd given so much. Until this point, all he'd done was take from her, something he'd fix if he got the chance.

Just as he was about to head back up the stairs behind Gregory, who'd found whatever he'd been searching for, a voice stopped him in his tracks.

"Robert!" it called, barely audible over the chaos. He turned to find Patricia, frantic and white as bone running toward him. "Robert, is Ginny here with you?"

"Of course not. She's up in her room with the kitten. Hannah. She's with Hannah."

"No, son, she's not. Oh, Lord above, we need to find her. Help me find her." A sob escaped the woman's chest, loud enough to silence the rest of the noise, the bustle. It was feral. The cry of a mother who'd lost her child.

Ginny. He'd left her up in her room with the kitten. Had he asked anyone to watch her when he chased after Lorelai? No, he didn't think so. *Ginny.* Where was she? Where was his daughter? Staring into the flames that devoured the barn—the barn she loved, filled with the animals she cherished—his heart sped wildly out of control.

Oh, God.

Where was his daughter?

CHAPTER NINE: THE FLAMES

Heat warmed Lorelai on her left side, a crackling sound in the distance calming her along with the warmth. With her eyes closed, she imagined she was on the coast of the Black Sea, where Robert had taken her and Ginny for one of their first trips. The sun had melted her from the outside in, while the blended drink he'd brought down for them—a pina colada he'd learned to make because it was her favorite—chilled her core. What a delicious blend of sensations.

Except now, things were different. She wasn't there, along the shore. There wasn't a drink in her hand. No laughter from Ginny as she splashed along the shoreline.

Instead of the smell of briny sea air, there was smoke.

It filled her nostrils, seemed to consume her. Something was on fire. Something close. A voice she recognized was calling out, but it was too faint, too far away for her to hear. She would just wait until it got closer.

She couldn't move anyway. Why couldn't she move? What was wrong? Her eyelids fluttered and light danced around her, penetrating her half-closed lids. It was orange, luminous.

The voice got closer, and she finally recognized it. It

was Robert. Her lover. Or at least he was. She'd broken up with him, hadn't she? Or had she? She couldn't recall. Something had broken her concentration, pulled her away.

The fire. There was a fire. In her barn.

Her eyes opened and she saw Robert running frantically alongside the barn, now completely engulfed in flames.

Oh, God. Everything she'd worked for was turning to ash. She sat up but was pushed back down by a strong hand.

"You've got to rest, miss. You've taken in a lot of smoke and we need to get you checked out."

"No. My barn. My horses."

"Your horses all got out safe. Now, please lie down and rest. We'll get you to the hospital as soon as we get the okay from the King. As soon as they find his daughter."

His daughter.

Ginny.

She was *missing?*

Oh, no.

No, no no.

"She's out there?"

"We're not sure. We have a team looking for her, and…"

Lorelai didn't wait to hear what the man had to tell her. In a flash, she was up off the stretcher she'd been lying on, sprinting toward the flames, toward Robert.

She could make out his cries now that she was close.

"Ginny! Jesus, please come out. Please be okay. *Ginny!"*

She fled along the wreckage of her barn, her desperation to find the young girl the only thing keeping her from teetering off the edge of a cliff. Everything she owned, everything she'd worked for was gone.

Obliterated.

Her memories, her past, her future were ash and smoke.

But none of that mattered if they couldn't find Ginny.

When she rounded a corner, she ran headlong into Robert.

"What are you doing up? You, you…" A sob finished his thoughts and Lorelai thought she might split in two right there. But she had to be strong for him. She'd lost so much, but he stood to lose everything if they didn't work together.

"I'm fine. Just a little smoke. We need to find Ginny. I need to help."

He only nodded, tears streaming down his face.

"Let's try the north barn."

"You think—?"

"I think she'll follow the kittens and horses. Besides, that's where Billie Jean is.

"You actually think she might… she might be okay?" The break in his voice cracked the tough veneer Lorelai was trying to keep up for him.

She met his gaze and kept it. His eyes were more gray than blue, all stormy waters.

"I have to, Robert."

He nodded again, and she followed him as he took off in a sprint for the north barn and stables.

Please, please, please let her be okay.

"Ginny!" they yelled in unison.

The heat from the south barn singed Lorelai's skin where she was exposed. If the fire squad couldn't get it under control, this barn would be next. And then there was nothing to stop the fire from devouring the land between there and the palace.

Lorelai tore through the stalls like she had that first day she'd discovered someone who shouldn't be in her barn. Sweet, precious Ginny. If anyone belonged amongst the horses, the barn cats, the hounds, it was that little girl.

She had to be okay, she just had to.

"Ginny, are you here?" Lorelai's attempt to keep her voice even, controlled, was shot to heck. Fear consumed her, but she didn't want to spook the horses.

"Please, Ginny, if you're here, we need to talk to you. You aren't in trouble," she added. She turned to Robert, who was silent, all the color drained from his face. He stood in the middle of the barn, spinning in circles. She understood his panic. "Robert, I need you to start releasing the horses into the field. Can you do that?"

He nodded and methodically started releasing the bolts so the horses could leave. Giving him a task seemed to help, but he wouldn't be the same until he had his daughter in his arms. She had to make that happen for him. For herself as well. She would never forgive herself if anything happened to Ginny on her watch. Never.

Her legs moved her over to Billie Jean's stall, her heart beating out a silent prayer.

Please, please, please. Oh, please, please, please.

Billie Jean's eyes were wide, reflecting the fear Lorelai felt.

When Lorelai opened the gate, Billie Jean ran at full speed for the entrance to the barn, narrowly missing Robert. Lorelai wasted no time in turning over the blankets, tossing the wood chips, but nothing.

Ginny wasn't there.

That was her only hope, that Ginny had run to save Billie Jean when she saw the fire. Now, she was drained. Drained of hope, of ideas. She didn't know where to turn next, and she couldn't go back and face Robert empty-handed, she just couldn't.

"Oh, Jesus. Oh, *God*," Robert called from the medical stall. Lorelai's hands shook, her chest heaved, and tears came with the force of a summer storm, hot and unrelenting. Her body propelled her toward his voice, but her mind told her to be prepared for the worst.

When she rounded the corner, her mind flashed back to the first day she'd heard a cry in her barn and worried someone was in trouble—someone who had no business being by her horses. Since then, she'd fallen in love with that little girl as much as she'd fallen in love with the horses. It was a relationship that grew each day, and it fulfilled Lorelai. Without it, she was no longer sure who she was.

It was this thought that sent a bubble of laughter up her stomach, through her chest, along her throat when she found herself face to face with the same scene as the day she'd met Lorelai.

There, on the ground, was a perfectly fine, if not a little dirty, Ginny. She was surrounded by kittens, a jug of milk from the house off to the side, three bowls filled with the liquid in a half-circle in front of her.

She squealed with pleasure when a kitten ran from the corner of the barn and jumped in her lap.

"Look, Daddy! I saved all the kitties!"

Lorelai wiped her cheeks, another peal of laughter escaping her throat that ached under the strain of the past hour. She looked at Robert, who was sobbing openly, his chest heaving as he struggled to catch his breath.

Ginny was fine, and she would be okay. Nothing else mattered.

Robert went to her, wrapped her in his strong arms, leaving Lorelai alone, watching the scene as a stranger would. An emptiness consumed her, brought her back to their conversation before they'd discovered the fire now that Ginny was safe.

Robert had argued Lorelai belonged with them, with him, but even at that moment, he'd forgotten about her. It was all the proof she needed to stay the course she'd set for herself just hours before. She needed to let him go, let him be the father and leader he was meant to be.

"Ginny, we need to get you back to the house. It's dangerous down here. The fire could hurt you, or worse," Robert said, tears still streaming down his face as he held his daughter.

"Daddy, I'm not leaving them here. They could get burned."

He only nodded, all fight from him gone. Lorelai

understood—what were a few extra kittens when Ginny was safe from harm?

"Okay, let's gather them up and head home."

"I'll help," Lorelai said, picking up an orange tabby from the barn floor and dusting her off.

"That won't be necessary," Robert replied, his voice curt. He snatched the kitten from her, turning his back again.

What? He wouldn't look at her, wouldn't give her even a sideways glance. His voice was hard as stone, cold as it, too. What had she done, other than tell him what she wanted, what she needed to do for her career? She'd done him a favor, hadn't she?

"Isn't Lory-lai coming with us?" Ginny asked.

Lorelai had gotten a handle on her emotions when Ginny was found, but now, her lungs burned with rejection, the heat spilling over her cheeks.

"She isn't, honey. She needs to be here, where she belongs."

She did, that was true, but why did it sound like she was banished the way he said it?

"No, Daddy, she belongs with me and you and the kitties. Don't be a meanie." Ginny wrestled out of Robert's grasp and ran to Lorelai. She threw herself at Lorelai's feet. Lorelai didn't know who was hurt more by Robert's dismissal of her—Lorelai or Ginny.

"Ginny, you need to—" he started, but never got the chance to finish. Whether that was a stay of execution or prolonging the inevitable remained to be seen.

"Your Grace," a member of the fire squad interrupted. "Oh, I'm glad you found your daughter. But you're going to want to see this."

Lorelai followed, not caring whether Robert wanted her there or not. This was her barn that was decimated, dammit. She had a right to know why, or how.

The squad leader led her and Robert to where the remains of the barn lay, smoke and ash and four concrete pillars. Nothing else. Not a shred of what her father had built remained. Every scrap of memories she'd brought over from New York was nothing more than rubble amongst the rest; it lay in black and charred ruin. Worse yet, she was homeless. Robert had kicked her out because she didn't accept his iteration of what her life should look like, and her apartment was gone.

How, after all this time, all her losses, was she back at the start again? And worse off, because the home she'd always assumed would take her back in had shunned her just as it had when she was a young adult.

She supposed she could ask Gregory to stay with him, but he was in the middle of his own drama. Lord, could this situation get any more hopeless? She was close to spiraling, spinning out of control, but she couldn't. Not yet. She needed to make sure her horses were cared for, moved to the pasture on the east end of the castle where the old stables were kept as backup.

Like it or not, they were all she had now.

While the squad leader talked to Robert in hushed whispers, Lorelai's glance was pulled to the edge of the wreckage. There, on the periphery, was her father's table, or what was left of it. She walked over to it, surveyed the damage. One whole side was charred, smoke still wafting off the remaining wood in little tufts. One of the three legs was nothing more than a stub.

That was how Lorelai felt—like a burnt, barely-standing being who was missing a limb.

She stumbled back to where Robert stared down at the dirt, kicking at it like he might unearth some hidden treasure that would make this all okay.

The squad leader was gone, and Robert wouldn't meet her gaze.

"What?" she asked. All pretense was gone—he deserved none of her empathy anymore. She was the one who'd lost everything, and he hadn't even considered her losses with her yet.

"You got what you wanted."

She let her chin drop, her mouth hanging open as if on a loose hinge.

"Excuse me?" she asked. Her voice was a full octave higher than normal, the frustration and disbelief adding an operatic pitch to every word. "How can you stand there and tell me minutes after a fire claimed almost everything I ever loved, ever owned, and lost the rest because of my ambition, that I got what I wanted? You callous prick!"

Robert didn't flinch. She wanted him to yell back, to make her feel something other than the exquisite loss she'd endured, the pain of defeat that threatened to bowl her over.

"I understand. And I'm sorry you're upset."

Upset? He was sorry she was *upset?* Had this man ever wanted for anything? Ever lost anything he couldn't replace immediately with his innumerable wealth and power? Her esteem for him fell as quickly as if she'd dropped it off the Empire State Building. Screw him and the horse he stomped on her heart with.

"You're a real national treasure, Robert. Would you care to elaborate on how exactly I'm being handed my dreams on a silver, charbroiled platter?"

Her voice had passed shrill a few minutes ago and was in vicious territory now.

"I fired Simon. I just got off the phone with him."

"So, how does this news build me a new apartment to sleep in tonight? Give my horses a place to bunk when the weather drops below zero next week? Because, unless Simon getting fired brings me those things, it's pretty useless to me at the moment, wouldn't you think?"

"I guess."

"Oh, good. You guess. Why did you fire your golden boy, anyway?"

Robert was back to kicking the charcoal-covered dirt.

"He, um, he started the fire. Then left."

Lorelai's mouth flew back open. The chill of the air

cooled the back of her throat that was still raw from the smoke.

"He *what?* Are you telling me this is *arson?*" She shivered, nothing to do with being cold.

"They don't think so. He tossed a still-lit cigarette, but the fire squad doesn't believe it's any more than negligence. Still, he was careless enough that I don't trust him running my hunt."

"Your hunt?" The one emotion that could shove the fear and grief from the night out of her system flooded it. Anger. She wanted to hurt Robert. Make him feel what it was like to lose something.

"Yes. This is still my property. I haven't cashed any of your checks, as you so cleverly discovered."

"But the deed. You signed it over to me."

"I didn't. I wanted to keep your checks aside, gift them with the barn back to you in three years, when the contract stipulates the deed would transfer to you. Then you'd have enough working capital to maintain it independently. But now it looks like that's a good thing since the liability falls to the kingdom to rebuild. I'll make sure the checks are returned to you and the contract reflects the damages and my culpability. Lorelai, I am offering you the job of stable manager if you want it, and it would come with the hunt. See? Everything you wanted."

He had the audacity to smile at her. With teeth and everything. She wanted to punch him right in the perfect pearly whites.

Her hands shook as she balled them into fists, prepared to do battle. At the last minute though, the effects of the fire caught up with her and her will to fight, to do anything other than sleep, evaporated.

"Don't do me any favors," she told him. "I've got an offer back in New York with my old hunt. Consider this my three-week notice." She walked away, afraid that he might call her back, offer her just enough to stay.

Her name on his lips might just be enough. Or would

have the day before, but not anymore.

The sobs came fast and heavy as soon as she was out of earshot of Robert. They wracked her chest, her shoulders feeling the burden of weightlessness that came with losing everything in one night. Her job, her family, her barn, her memories of her father. All of it was ash, dust. The only thing holding her upright was imagining buying a ticket, getting on a plane, and flying as far from her home as she could before starting to come at it from the other side of the globe.

Aldonia had raised her, given her memories and a passion for the hunt, for horses. But it had also claimed her heart. That was before smashing it into a million pieces and taking everything she loved from her in a single swipe.

Sniffling, wiping the dampness from her cheeks, she straightened her shoulders. No matter what it cost her, she still had her health, and she'd dig her passion out from the ashes and wipe it off.

She'd done it before.

Robert had come close to being her end when she was younger, and though this time was infinitely worse because she knew what she would be missing, she wouldn't let him drag her down again. No, King Robert of Aldonia would rue the day he let Lorelai slip from his grasp. He'd never find a better rider, a more compassionate horse trainer; not in Europe, anyway.

Nor would he find a better fit for him and as a co-parent to Ginny.

As she made her way up to Gregory's suite, she tossed a sideways glance to the lit room that had been hers until that evening.

A chill wrapped around Lorelai's shoulders, and she sent a silent prayer the same chill would find its way to the empty side of Robert's bed that night, to remind him that Lorelai wasn't the only one who lost something that night.

They both had, and Lorelai had the feeling both of them would feel the sting of loss long after the new dawn had risen.

CHAPTER TEN: THE MISTAKE

Robert peered out the window, his shoulder against the cold glass. Frost dappled the roofline. Winter wasn't too far off, now.

Crap. He wanted the construction of the barn to be done before the first snow hit, but it didn't look like that was going to happen. The framing was done, but they were still a long way off from getting the plumbing stubbed out, not to mention the drywall and electrical.

He thought being King might have inspired the necessary motivation for the construction crew to pick up the pace, but he couldn't have foreseen the stall in lumber because of the trade embargo with Russia. Now he was staring at a half-built barn, and not one construction worker was in sight.

The only movement came from Lorelai's constant vigil of the work site. Every morning, Robert watched from his glass-enclosed perch as she stalked the edge of the lumber, kicked at the dirt that was still stained with black ash. She ran her hands along the western edge of the framing, likely imagining what it would look like when it was done.

He knew because he did the same thing. He'd walk the corridors of the palace and wonder if the crimson that caught his eye on a framed piece of art would look good on the apartment walls. He'd watch Ginny with her stable kittens and his mind would trail off to when he could bring the horses back from the other side of his property.

And then there were his daughter's heartachingly persistent questions he couldn't answer. Ginny asked every day when she could go riding with Lorelai, when she could take Billie Jean out. She wanted to know why Lorelai didn't sleep over anymore, why she didn't make them her special pancakes in the morning.

He wished he had easy answers for her, for the similar questions that plagued him, but there wasn't anything easy about this. And there wouldn't be—not without Lorelai there to give him the answers.

She wasn't coming to do that anytime soon—he'd made sure of that when he'd all but ousted her the night her world had fallen around her in flames and ash.

God, how he'd been wrong…

Because it was still her barn, they were still her horses, at least in his eyes.

Not that it meant anything to her anymore. She was leaving in a week for New York and there wasn't a thing he could do about it. Oh, how he'd tried. He'd sent flowers, jewelry, heck even a new dress that was worth half of what the barn rebuild cost was.

But nothing.

She hadn't so much as said hello to him since the fire despite the fact that she was staying with her brother and his wife in the adjacent suite to Ginny's. He passed her in the hall every day on his way to the office, and her eyes would fall, her shoulders shrugged away from him. He was worse than invisible to her—he was the plague.

What would it take to get her to see that he messed up, that he was sorry?

A knock came from the door to his suite, rousing him from his self-deprecating thoughts.

"Yeah," he replied. The door opened and Philip came

in, brandishing a mug in each hand.

"Hey there, brother. I figured you could use one of these." Philip handed over one of the mugs. Robert inhaled deeply, the aromatic scent of vanilla mixed with coffee beans waking him up more than the steaming liquid would. He hadn't slept well in two weeks. It would take more than just a cup of joe to get him back to anything near functioning.

"Thanks. Smells good."

"How's it looking out there?"

Robert looked out again at the barn, and his heart sank. It wasn't going well. Nothing was.

"Eh. It's going. Just not as quickly as I'd hoped."

"I wanted to talk to you about that, actually. I was at Gregory's last night and Lor—" Philip stopped himself and coughed. Robert rolled his eyes and waved for Philip to continue. Everyone had been walking on eggshells on his behalf and he was sick of it. He could stomach her name, at least. "Sorry. But um, his *sister* came up with something pretty interesting."

"Okay. I'm interested." Because the only thing worse than Lorelai not talking to him was failing her by not giving her back her father's barn. It was rightly hers, and even when she went back to New York, he wanted her to have what was hers when she came home.

"Take a look at these. She pointed out that Russia needs access to the port in the Black Sea for trade and might be willing to negotiate a deal on lumber."

Well, heck. Why hadn't his advisors thought of that? Worse yet, why hadn't *he*? Sure, he was a little preoccupied with where Lorelai was going when she went out in the afternoons on her rides, and maybe how she was feeling, and okay, he really couldn't get his mind off what would get her attention back on him. But he was *the king*. He needed to start acting like it.

"That could work. Let me see the numbers."

Philip passed him the papers he'd come with. Robert

rifled through them, his interest growing with each page he flipped. Philip was right—the numbers worked. He could make some calls and get some progress going on the embargo.

"This is pretty great. Sometimes I think you should have been the one to run the show."

"You tease, but I'd be pretty awesome as king. Send Georgia the keys to the mountain pass. Free wine for everyone."

Robert laughed.

"I think Dad tried that one when he was first crowned. A week of drunk advisors and a bunch of stray Georgians really set him back a bit."

"I'll bet. But you know in all seriousness I had nothing to do with this idea. I'm just the messenger."

Robert sighed. He ran his hands through his hair and looked through the window. Lorelai was walking back up the path to the castle, a look of pain etched on her face. That he was partially the cause of that cinched his chest tight enough it was hard to breathe.

"I know. Tell her thanks. This'll help more than just the rebuild. We can get started on the rehabilitation center."

"Why don't you tell her yourself? She's actually got a few ideas that could help us."

"Okay, that's all well and good, but what about the fact that she's leaving for New York?"

"She doesn't want to go. She just doesn't think she has a choice. You aren't exactly paving the way for her to stay, are you?"

Robert paced the length of the window. He pointed his finger at Philip, his lips pressed tight together. He wagged his finger feeling not unlike his mother at that moment.

"How haven't I? I gave her the barn, I offered for her to live with me, travel with the crown. I let her be around Ginny. And since the fire, I've sent her dozens of roses, earrings, a necklace. I sent her a gown that cost a fortune.

But sure, I haven't done anything to show her I want her to stay."

Robert hated that his voice came out as a whine. But his brother didn't have any idea what he was talking about. He'd done his best and failed. Period. It sucked for all parties involved, Lorelai the most. That was what hurt the most.

"Yeah. Sounds like you really know the woman. It's a wonder she didn't just roll over and let you plan her whole life out for her."

"Hey. That's not fair."

"No, it isn't. Not for her, anyway."

"Okay, Mr. Know-It-All. Then what would you have me do?" Robert crossed his arms over his chest, annoyed. Who did Philip think he was? Just because he'd come out of his funk and let Aurelia in his life, suddenly he was the expert?

"Well, for starters, ask yourself what she wants."

"That's easy. She wants the barn."

"Duh. What else? Did she seem happy you gave it to her as a gift?"

Robert stopped his pacing, his hands on his hips. He went to answer, but the truth came hard against his chest.

"Um, no. She wanted to buy it. I, uh, think she was maybe a bit offended I hadn't cashed her checks."

"Okay, now we're getting somewhere. Why was she upset?"

Why was she? That was the sticking point. Robert thought she would have been overjoyed to have all the money saved. He could afford it, and she couldn't, plain and simple.

"I don't know. I mean, she wanted to run the hunt, so I thought she could use the money she saved to get that off the ground."

"Didn't you hire Simon, the guy who started the fire?"

"Yeah. So she could run it eventually."

"Ah, eventually. Let me see if I have this right. She

could take the money she was giving you that you were secretly keeping for her, and run a hunt you gave to someone else? And she didn't take you out back and make love to you right then and there?"

Robert scowled. His brother had always teased him, but this was below the belt. It was about Lorelai. And dang if Philip might be right.

"Fine. But what about the gifts? I'm trying to say I'm sorry for all the, you know, other stuff. Why isn't it enough? What else can I do?"

"She's not a flower and jewelry kinda girl, Robert. Women aren't one-size-fits-all. What would show her you understand her? Because that's the only way you're getting her attention. She wants to be seen, you know. For who she is, for what makes her special to you."

"For who she is." Robert thought about that. Because she was special to him. More than he'd let her know, and that was a gross oversight on his part. "Wait. I think I have it."

Robert went to his bedroom. He opened the oak chest that held everything dear to him and rifled through the boxes of photos until he found what he was looking for. He pulled a small silk satchel from the back and opened it.

The small wooden horse Lorelai's dad carved for him rested in his hand, a talisman that represented everything he loved, Lorelai included. In it, he also saw everything Lorelai loved and lost in the fire.

Himself included.

"What about this?" he asked Philip, holding up the small figurine. Robert took his brother's wide grin as a good sign that he was on the right track.

"Didn't her dad…?"

"Yeah. When Mom and Dad…"

"Oh."

Robert cleared his throat and Philip coughed.

"So, you think it'll work?"

"I do. But that can't be it, you know. She took a job in

New York. A little wooden horse isn't going to fix that. You've got to make The Big Gesture."

"The *what*?"

Robert looked at his brother like he had two heads. What the heck was he talking about? A big gesture? How big? He'd already bought out the most expensive and exclusive jeweler. How much bigger could he go?

"The big gesture. You know, where you let her know she's the one you want in a way that screams it from the rooftops."

"What kind of thing would count as a big gesture?"

Philip laughed and set the papers he'd brought with him on the large coffee table. He patted his brother on the shoulder and made his way back to the entrance of the suite.

"That, older brother, is for you to figure out. But you can't do it by thinking about what Marjorie would have wanted, or anyone else for that matter. You have to think about Lorelai, put yourself in her shoes. And then give her exactly what she needs but can't do herself."

"Well, crap, Philip. When did you get to be so smart?"

"Since I almost lost everything I ever cared about."

"Oh yeah. Aurelia."

Philip nodded. "Don't worry. It'll come to you. You love her, right?"

"I do. So much."

"Then don't let her go." Philip left and shut the door behind him, leaving Robert alone with his thoughts.

Robert remembered when his brother had gone after Aurelia when she'd moved to New York. He'd shown up at her doorstep and brought her and the baby she was carrying back to Aldonia, but first he'd told her the truth—all of it. It was scary for all of them, most of all Philip, but it was one heck of a gesture. Robert preferred not to fly back to win Lorelai's heart back, though. It would be better if he could reach her before she moved back to the States.

So, how was he supposed to do this?

He'd figure it out. He had to. Because the alternative wasn't something he would let happen.

Until he could get a plan fleshed out, he at least had something to keep himself busy. He fished his phone out of his pocket and called his chief advisor.

"Petre. Get me the ambassador to Russia. I've got something he has to hear."

Six days later, Robert watched as the last of the siding on the barn was painted. He'd gone with as close to the rust-brown as he could since Lorelai hadn't given him any indication she wanted to choose a color. Or talk about anything else related to Robert. She had come around and started talking to Ginny, but that only made things worse. She'd leave in the next two days, and then he wouldn't be the only one that was crushed. His daughter would be, too. And he couldn't have that—things were strained enough with Ginny since she seemed to consider him at fault for her lack of riding and Lorelai's impending departure. She wasn't wrong.

He was starting to feel like it was hopeless. He had a new barn for her, sure, but other than that, the only thing he had to offer her was a figurine of a horse that could fit in the palm of his hand. Not exactly a grand gesture. To make matters worse, he would have to push back the hunting season because he hadn't hired on a new huntsman. He was still—idiotically, he knew—holding out hope that Lorelai would take the position.

Maybe if he offered to help wrangle the horses and bring them back to the barn? It seemed like the only thing he could do that would put him close enough to her so he could explain himself and apologize. It might get him back in good graces with Ginny, too. His own daughter wouldn't speak to him about anything other than her plans for the day.

Ugh. How had so much become muddled in so short a time?

"Your Grace?"

Robert shook his head, cleared his throat.

"Come in." He turned to see his Irish cook and house manager, Patricia, arms crossed over her ample chest. A friendly face was just what he needed. "Ah, Patricia. How's Ginny behaving for you today?" Ginny was in the kitchen helping Patricia prepare the Sunday meal for the family. He wanted his daughter to have all the knowledge she would need to run a household someday, especially since the kingdom would be hers someday.

"She's fine, but her father's being a daft idiot."

Robert all but stumbled back. Patricia had known him since he was born, had worked for his family even longer than that. But she'd never spoken like that to him. To his reckless brother, sure. But not to Robert, the more responsible of the two.

"Excuse me?" he spat. Anger built in his chest, but he swallowed what he could down into the pit of his stomach. She wasn't the reason he was pissed. He was mad at himself for his utter ineptitude when it came to fixing the issue with Lorelai.

"Oh, son. You're the smartest man I know, and you can lead this country to greatness with both your hands tied behind your back. But when it comes to women, you know exactly squat."

A mirthless laugh escaped his chest. "Why don't you tell me how you really feel, Patricia?"

"Oh, I'm just getting started, young man. Sit."

He was teasing her; he certainly hadn't meant for her to tell him how she really felt about him, but despite being the king and drastically outranking the woman, he obeyed and sat down on top of his silk comforter. He might be the ruler of the country, but she'd always known how to make him feel like a little boy who'd screwed up yet again.

"Okay, Patricia, what have I done this time?"

"You don't tell me when to talk, Robert. I'll tell you when I'm good and ready." She paced along the window ledge he'd spent most of the past three weeks staring out of. "You like this view, hmmm?"

Crap. He'd been caught creepily stalking his ex-something or other. Could he even call her a girlfriend if she'd never been his to begin with?

He nodded.

"You sit up here all day while she plans to fix your barn, your stables, reintegrate your horses, is that correct? And you don't do anything to help."

He nodded again, the strain of her astuteness sitting heavy on his shoulders. That last sentence wasn't phrased as a question.

"That sounds about right."

"Well, then it's time for you to get off that lazy rump of yours and do something of value."

"What do you suggest?"

She shook an angry finger in his face. Though the gesture could be considered comical, especially since he wasn't five years old anymore, he didn't find anything about his situation funny.

"Don't you get fresh with me, Robert. You're about to ruin a lot of lives if you don't act like the man your father raised. Starting with getting that little girl of yours out of my kitchen."

"What did she do?"

"Besides nearly burning the place down, she hates it there. She isn't meant to do what I do, Robert, and to assume she is because she's a young lady is insulting. To her, and to you, frankly. It undermines the intelligence I know is bumbling around in there, somewhere." She tapped his forehead firmly before recrossing her arms.

Wow. She always spoke her mind, but the way she was speaking to him was personal. She was being mean.

"She's four. What should she be doing, then?"

"Do you not have any idea what makes your daughter happy, Robert? Because I believe that you do, but you're too stubborn to do anything about it because it would involve getting out of your own way and apologizing to Lorelai. Which is my next argument, so I won't say too much about that until we've finished with Ginny."

"Oh, goody. If you've got such a good handle on what my preschooler should spend her time learning, why don't you just come out with it? I've got enough problems without worrying that I'm screwing her life up, too."

He was tired of this game. Twice in a week he'd been accused of not knowing anything about the women in his life, and judging by the fact that neither his daughter nor Lorelai was speaking to him, that wasn't incorrect. That didn't mean he had any clue what to do about it, though.

"She belongs in the stables."

Huh? The truth hit him across the forehead as thickly as if Patricia had walloped him on the head again. Patricia was right. Each time he mentioned the kittens or horses, Ginny's face would light up, a smile of pure pleasure on her face. But there hadn't been stables to send her to until that afternoon.

"Okay. Consider this her last day with you in the kitchen, but that doesn't mean she'll find a place in the barn, either."

"And why not?"

"There isn't anyone there to teach her. Simon was fired, and well, you know about Lorelai. So until I can get a new barn manager in there, Ginny will have to find something else on the property to fill her time after school."

"Are you really that stubborn that you would cut your nose to spite your face?"

"Patricia, I love you like my own mother, but I've never understood that saying before. What are you talking about?"

"I'm talking about Lorelai. When and how do you propose to get her back?"

"Who says I am going to?"

"If you weren't thinking about it, son, then you're as

ignorant as I feared."

Robert sighed and ran his hands through his hair. He looked at the woman who'd helped raise him, a woman he couldn't hide his true feelings from. She knew him better than he knew himself.

"I have been. But I'm stuck. I have a little figurine her dad made for me and I was about to offer to help her wrangle the horses back to their new home. That's it. That's all I've got. Please help me, Pat. I don't want to lose her." The last four words came choked out on a sob he neither expected nor could contain.

Patricia sat on the bed next to Robert. She placed a hand on his knee and gave it a maternal pat.

"Oh, son. As long as you're breathing, there's hope for you. You won't lose her if you're honest. She loves you. God help me, I'm not sure why any of those women love any of you, but they do."

The sob turned into a chortle.

"I'm not sure why they do, either. Was it this difficult for Philip and Aurelia?"

"Worse. He let the poor girl get all the way home and almost had to drag her back here against her will. It was a Greek tragedy before he got through to her."

Tears rolled down his cheeks, but laughter rolled off his chest.

"Well, that's encouraging. At least I've not let Lorelai actually cross the Atlantic with my ineptitude. Not yet, anyway."

"And Gregory wasn't much better. By all accounts, you're ahead of the game, but let's try not to even the playing field, shall we?"

Robert shook his head.

"Not on my agenda. So how do I reach her when all I have in my pocket is helping relocate a dozen horses?"

"Well, you'll interview her for the position of huntsman, and you'll send her a new contract that lets her earn the property back. She's worked her whole life,

Robert. Nothing has come to that girl for free, not especially anything worth having. You could learn a thing or two from her on that account."

"Ha ha. I can do that, but why would she accept either? I've got nothing to give her to trust me. To make her listen to what I have to say."

"You have the horse."

"That hardly seems enough for all that's at risk for her. I want her to know if she stays, she won't have to worry that it'll all come crashing down around her."

"Darling, you can't guarantee that any more than you can assure her the birds will come back in the Spring. You can hope all day long, but it will still be out of your control, won't it?"

"Then how does anyone do anything and not worry it'll get screwed up along the way?"

"Faith, my boy. We all have faith that those we love will do the best they can and be there when our worlds fall apart. Because they will fall apart. There's no stopping that—that's life. You have to show her you'll be there to help her rebuild not just the barn but her memories as well. She lost almost everything in that fire, Robert. It wasn't just the building. It was her childhood."

"All I can help with is the building. The rest was all personal stuff. Clothes, photos. Those can't be replaced."

Robert's chest constricted. If he lost everything from his folks, all the mementos, gifts, he didn't know what he'd do. He'd be crushed. He understood how she must feel, but still felt lost about how to help.

"Can't they? Robert, you and your brother know we live in the age of technology. Surely there's something out there on that big ol' web that could help you out?"

"Yes. Yes, you're right."

"I know, son. I'm just glad you do, too."

That shred of an idea flitting around in his head acted as a catalyst, spinning whatever gear had been asleep at the wheel. He saw her small apartment in perfect clarity, every photo of every horse imprinted on his mind as if he'd hung them himself. If he could find the photos on her social media, that would be perfect. Maybe Gregory could even share some of their father, their family.

He closed his eyes and saw the layout of the furniture, the paint, the pots and pans that hung from above the sink. It was all there, in his memory that refused to let even the smallest part of her pass by him unnoticed.

He could recreate it.

He could give her something that she'd thought was irreplaceable and see her world put back together. Knowing the smile it would bring to her face was all Robert needed. To heck if she didn't want him back afterward. Just so long as she was happy, so long as she had some piece of who she was back.

If anything, he owed her that as a friend. If she was never anything more than that to him, then that was just how things were. Screw it. He wasn't going to let that stop him from doing the right thing.

But wait. Something was missing. When he walked around the virtual recreation of her apartment he'd imagined, there was a central piece in her walkway he couldn't place. What had been there.

Suddenly, his eyes popped open.

The table. Her father's table that he and Philip had pulled from the fire before it was burned to a crisp. It had survived the fire with only slightly charred edges, but had disappeared between the fire and finding a missing Ginny. Where had it gone? Philip wouldn't have let anything happen to it, but Robert needed that piece if his plan was going to work.

He got up from the bed, only to jump out of his skin when a small cough came from behind him.

Patricia sat there, a smug smile on her face.

Crap. He'd forgotten she was still there. And of course, she'd be pleased with herself. She'd successfully meddled with his brother's and Gregory's relationships until they'd ended up with the loves of their lives. He was well aware that was what was happening to him, but he didn't care.

They'd all needed a swift kick in the ass when it came to getting out of their own way and being there for the women who made their lives fuller, richer than all the trade and gold in Europe could. He owed Patricia a debt he didn't think he could ever repay. But he'd sure as hell try when this was all over.

Whether or not it ended with Lorelai in his life.

"Okay, okay. I'll admit it. You're right. You're always right. But I still need your help to pull this off."

"Sure, hun. Just tell Patricia here what you need and I'll make sure you get it."

"Do you know anything about her father's table?"

"Her father's table? The one from the fire? What about it?"

"I need to know where it is."

"Your brother had it moved to the gardener's shed to be repaired."

"Do you know if he started to fix it?"

"I don't believe so. He's been busy with preparing the suite to welcome their son. Aurelia is due in less than a week."

"I know. I can't believe it. Okay, well, I'm going to take that on personally. Do you think you can get Lorelai to the barn with Ginny tomorrow night? That should be enough time to take care of everything. Oh, and I'll need to commandeer the maintenance staff. Do you mind?"

"Not a bit, Your Grace. I'll take care of Ginny, too. Just anywhere but the kitchen."

Robert laughed, feeling lighter than he had in years. He had a good feeling about this. It might not be enough to convince Lorelai she could trust him, but it would be enough to show her he loved her. That would be plenty.

"That's perfect. Thank you." He kissed the top of her head, wrapped her in a hug that all but smothered her. "For everything. You're the best, Patricia."

"I know. Now get out of here. You've got work to do, son."

That he did. His mind whirred like the start of an engine at the International Speedway. He'd start in the gardening shed, which was really more of an elaborate greenhouse, then make his way to the apartment.

On the way, though, he'd call Gregory to see what he could do about the photos.

Excited about his plan falling into place, Robert rushed through changing his clothes and headed down to the shed.

He wasn't worried about running into her there, but he needed something or someone to get her away from the barn when phase two of his plan came to fruition. Aside from meals and packing for her move, she'd spent every single minute overseeing the reconstruction.

That was the last shred of hope he clung to.

If Lorelai was still that invested in the building of the barn, then she still had a connection to it, to him. She wasn't gone yet. It meant he still had time to convince her to stay, even if it was a fool's errand.

He was a fool for her, and he was going to take advantage of every chance he got before she left for good, taking his heart with her.

CHAPTER ELEVEN: THE PLAN

Lorelai inhaled deeply, letting the cool air infiltrate her lungs and spread to her extremities. When she released the breath, the desire to look back at Robert's window—what had been her window until recently—left with it.

He was gone.

It was time she faced the facts. Sure, he'd spent the better half of the past three weeks sending her gifts and building back her barn, but he'd never once stopped her to talk.

To find out how she was doing.

To ask her if she wanted to help him decorate the new apartment.

To ask her to stay.

She'd avoided him and the new barn the whole day prior when he'd brought in new furniture, the painting crew, and what she assumed were decorations more befitting a royal apartment. Everything was under sheets and tarps, a veil of secrecy around an already close-lipped man.

Oh, well. It wasn't hers anymore—any of it. Let him do with his property how he saw fit.

Robert was acting like a coward, and she didn't have

the energy to drag him along, teach him how to be in an adult relationship. He really had no clue what Lorelai wanted, who she was.

And the jewelry? Please. It was gaudy, expensive. It was Marjorie's taste, not hers. Ugh. Did he really think she was anything like that hussy?

He did. Of course, he did.

He assumed that much at least when he told her he'd "let" her tag along with him when he traveled. Ha! Like that was even something she'd be interested in. She wanted to be with him, sure, but she knew, appreciated even, that they were different. That their lives would lead them separate ways as much as it seemed hell-bent on throwing them onto the same path. If they'd ever stood a chance, he would have had to have seen that she needed to be there, in the stables, with her horses. Not adorning his arm like one of the fancy baubles he'd sent her.

And then he'd gone and thrown Ginny in the kitchen because it would teach her how to run a household of her own someday. Oh, good God. The man knew nothing.

Less than nothing about women, especially the women who loved him most.

Fine. Let him self-destruct by shoving them all away. He'd be alone and with no one to lament that he'd pissed away all the best people in his life.

Her breathing hitched in her chest, and a small sob got stuck in her throat.

Crap. She was letting herself get worked up again. That hadn't done her a bit of good the weeks since the fire, and it certainly wouldn't over the next few days as she finalized her move. Today was her last day officially employed, and she had to get used to that.

She ran her hand along the smooth pine that had been shipped in special from Georgia, the roofing from Russia. It looked good, far better than the original barn that was starting to wear before it had been claimed by fire. Robert had done well. The call to Russia to open up trade again was the right one to make.

He'd taken her idea and ran with it, to great success, apparently. That was the real rub. Yes, she wanted to be the head huntsman, and yes, she wanted to manage and run her own barn someday. But she was smart, saw things about her home country that were flawed, and she had ideas on how to change them. She could be more than arm candy—she could have been Robert's partner, helping him guide his country into the next hundred years successfully and prosperously.

But, no, he'd forced her hand, not given her any other option than to fill Marjorie's shoes. And that was worse than not offering anything at all because it meant she had to turn everything down, including her barn.

Her horses.

Her job.

Her first love.

Her fingers slid along the new stable doors that would house everything she loved, all her memories, but wouldn't be part of her future. At that point, she didn't know if any barn would be.

She hadn't told anyone—not even Gregory—that she was moving back to New York blind. It was a lie, what she'd angrily told Robert about having a job offer. In reality, her position had been taken by an American from Arizona who had more experience than anyone Lorelai had ever met when it came to scheduling and running hunts. A Meghan something or other.

The owner and operator had promised Lorelai would be the first in line if anything came up, but at the moment, he didn't have anything to offer her.

Crap. Crap. Crap. If she had a shred of dignity left, she'd eat crow and tell Robert she was sorry, and could she still have the job? She didn't need the barn to be hers, but she could use a roof over her head that would come with a generous paycheck. Because in a serious twist of fate too cruel for Lorelai to consider too deeply, Robert hadn't hired anyone to take Simon's place.

Gregory gossiped to her it was because Robert was hoping she'd stay and take the job. But she hadn't heard squat from Robert himself, so how could she possibly be the one to open that can of worms?

She was used to chaos, to turning it into something she could work with, something that even resembled calm by the time she was done molding it, but this situation took that to an unhealthy level. How the heck had everything gotten so screwed up so quickly? One minute, she'd been playing house with the man she loved more than anything, and the next, her whole life had gone up in flames.

Literally.

Crap. Crap. Double crap.

She knew what she had to do, but that didn't mean she liked it. Not one bit.

Just as she was out of the doors of the new barn, the sunlight hitting her cheeks with a chill that belied the winter nipping at their heels, she ran headlong into Aurelia, knocking the petite woman to her butt in the dirt.

"Crap. I'm so sorry," she exclaimed, rushing to help Philip's wife back on her feet. "Are you okay? Is the baby…?"

Aurelia laughed. Lorelai didn't think she'd ever seen the woman less than effervescent, not even now, when she was days from giving birth and was knocked over by a wildebeest.

"I'm fine, thanks. There's nothing that could shake this baby out of his comfortable lounging in my stomach. I've half a mind to ask you to knock me a little harder so the little fella feels like coming out to join us."

"You're getting tired, huh?"

Lorelai's best friend, Jess, had given birth while she was in New York, and all Lorelai recalled was how exhausted her friend had been at the end of her pregnancy. She bent down to pick up the burlap sack Aurelia had been carrying, handing it back to the woman.

"Thanks. And yes. He doesn't seem willing to move an inch except to burrow further from where he needs to be. I made him too cozy, apparently, and now he's staying put."

Lorelai chuckled. "Not that I blame him. This winter's going to be a fierce one from what I've read."

"Not sorry you're going to miss it, huh?"

Lorelai sighed. "I'll miss it a lot, actually. More than I care to admit. But no, the snow and ice we're capable of producing up here aren't part of that list."

Aurelia put her hands on her hips, no small feat for a woman whose stomach loomed over the rest of her tiny figure that didn't look even a day into pregnancy.

"What did?"

"Excuse me?"

"What did make the list of things you're going to miss?"

Lorelai shifted her gaze to her feet. She didn't want to give voice to what topped her list, not when she'd worked so hard to forget about it, about him.

"Um, well, the horses, of course. And the summers preparing them for the hunting season. The hounds are smelly beasts, but I'll miss them, too. I do wish you and I would have had more time to get to know each other. But you can always take a break and come visit me in New York. Show me the good dive bars." She forged a smile that didn't quite reach her eyes. At that moment, it was the best she could do.

"That's it, huh? Nothing else makes the list?"

Lorelai caught the smug smile on the woman's face and ignored it. No way was she falling for that trap.

"Well, let's not forget Ginny, my new riding partner. She made me remember what I loved about riding, why I started in the first place. Noelle, too."

Lorelai's heart constricted and her chest tightened, laboring her breathing. There weren't words for how much she would miss Ginny. She'd told the truth about why, but that barely scratched the surface of all the little girl had meant to her.

Ginny was Lorelai's only experience being an aunt, or more, to a child. As it turned out, Lorelai liked being a maternal figure, and was quite good at it as well. Another cruel twist of fate that occurred too late for her to do anything about it.

Lorelai bit her lip and turned her gaze to the weak sun above her, staving off tears that threatened to fall.

"She's going to miss you, too. We all are. Especially Ginny. And her father."

Lorelai looked back down at Aurelia. Gone was the smirk, replaced by an authentic smile that seemed laced with the same pain Lorelai felt building in the pit of her stomach.

"He won't. He'll miss having someone around, but he'll find someone new, someone more his taste."

More his pace and lifestyle, too.

"He doesn't want anyone else, Lorelai. He wants you."

Lorelai frowned. She didn't want to hear this. Not when she'd built a wall to prevent just that sort of hope from infiltrating her defenses.

"No, he doesn't. He wants someone like Marjorie. Someone to look nice on his arm as he does all his royal king-thingys around the world. I'm not that person."

Aurelia placed her hand on Lorelai's shoulder. Lorelai met her gaze but didn't like what she saw there.

"Listen to me. I don't want to meddle in someone else's affairs, not especially when it took me forever to see what I'm asking you to in Robert with his brother. But I hate to think I could have done something and didn't. Because you two love each other, you're just both too stubborn to admit it."

Lorelai opened her mouth to reply. What did Aurelia know about her or her stubbornness? Aurelia shot her a look that shut her up before she could defend her own honor.

Fine. She'd listen. Worst case and she was still gone in a couple of days, no worse for the wear.

"He's been burned before, and I thought the guy would end up celibate and alone the rest of his life until you came along. You didn't just ignite a joy in him that I thought he'd lost, but you gave him a family that made him happier than I've ever seen him. Than Philip has ever seen him. But that doesn't mean he knows how to tell you."

Lorelai crossed her arms over her chest to hide the erratic breaths that came in short, machine-gun bursts. Crap, indeed. She wasn't expecting any of this and frankly didn't know what to do with the news.

"So what would you have me do? He hasn't so much as said hi to me in weeks."

"Stubborn. Like I said. But we can't get him to shut up about you, about needing you to stay. Not that we blame him—we'd all be crushed if you left. Who would take me horseback riding when this other stubborn little guy finally joins us?" Aurelia winked. Good gracious, she was just like her husband and brother-in-law—tenacious as heck. It warmed a place in Lorelai that she'd thought was dormant at best. It had been a while since anyone had fought for her, begged her to stick around. Even though at that moment she'd rather it had been a different member of the royal family.

"Why don't you just go talk to him, ask him how he's feeling? What's the worst that can happen?"

Lorelai tried not to imagine the actual worst thing, that similar to how he'd treated her in high school, he'd shrug her off as nothing more than an annoyance. She didn't think her heart could brave that again. Not now that she knew what his hands felt like on her skin, his lips tasted like on hers. She'd had all of him, and she didn't want to ever go back to the alternative.

It would kill her.

"Okay. But I'm coming to read you the riot act if you're wrong."

Aurelia broke into a grin that spread across her face. "Deal. I'll even help you pack if I'm wrong. And that's the best offer I can make when the couch with a plate of herring and ice cream is the alternative."

Lorelai couldn't help the grin that spread across her cheeks, nor the hope that spread from her heart through her chilled extremities. She was already tempted to swallow her pride and ask—beg if she was reduced to it—for her job back, but now she made the walk to the castle with her shoulders back, her chest inflated with the new injection of hope.

When she got up to the back doors of the castle, the entrance she used when she stayed with Robert, the guard let her in. His smile, subtle and kind, was disarming. Did everyone know something she didn't?

Her boots were silent on the stone floor, but her breath echoed off the walls. She was nervous, and try as she did to rein it in, she couldn't. This was her future. One way or another, a door would close tonight. One would leave her with everything she'd ever wanted, and more.

The other would leave her penniless in another country without hope of a job or a place to live. How the heck had she let herself get there, where those were her only two choices? Her father would have a field day with her decisions of late. He used to exhume the mantra that she should make choices that opened up opportunities for her, to ditch those that backed her into a corner.

Well, her back was to the wall now, wasn't it? She sighed. *Not the time, Lorelai. You need your strength now.*

Voices, low and hushed, trickled into the tall, narrow hallway. Her name floated out amongst other, less audible mumbling. What the…?

She took care to step softly and hold in her ragged breath to hear better. She recognized Robert's right away, but who was he was with? Two steps closer, as silent as she could be, she found herself against the barely cracked door.

Why was he talking about her? And why the heck did he feel the need to whisper in his own home? This didn't feel right, any of it. *Philip.* Robert was whispering secrets to Philip. And she had something to do with it. Um, no.

Against her better judgment, she pressed her ear to the small gap between the door and the wall. She shivered, a chill darting up her spine.

"And you're sure about this? About her?"

Her? Lorelai? Was Aurelia completely off base when she told Lorelai Robert wanted her to stay?

"I have to do this. Lorelai's a great mom to Ginny, and I don't want to give that up. Ginny would miss her. I know she would."

Lorelai took in a sharp breath of air.

What?

Ginny was the only reason Robert wanted her to stay?

He couldn't mean that. Could he? Aurelia had said…

Never mind what Aurelia told her. Because Robert had finally said how he really felt. He'd told her in so many ways, she'd just been too lovesick to listen. Growing up, he'd never noticed her, not once. When he finally did, he only saw her as a nanny to watch his daughter, who he hoped would magically transform into a trophy at night for him to take to royal functions. Ugh. Why hadn't she listened when he told her exactly how he saw her with his actions? Because the words themselves were infinitely worse.

The sting of rejection pushed out any of the hope that rose in Lorelai's chest, her heart. It curdled the love she felt for Robert, for her country, and turned it sour.

All she could see as she turned and ran were the blurred edges of her vision marred by tears that fell hot against her icy skin. The door had closed, leaving her alone in the cold to fend for herself. A sob escaped her throat as she ran past the guard, past the new stables she would never call home.

She was a fool to believe Robert could change and

accept her as a woman, a friend, a partner after all this time.

People didn't change, and the sooner she learned that, the sooner her heart could stop shattering into thousands of pieces.

CHAPTER TWELVE: THE RACE

Robert stopped mid-sentence. He held his breath, straining to hear outside his suite.

"Did you hear that?"

Philip shook his head and pulled from the bottle of imported American beer his wife kept on hand.

"Hear what? Hey, have you tried this swill? Americans do some things right. NASCAR, for instance. But I think beer should be left to the Dutch."

"I heard something outside the door. A woman, I think."

"I think you're hearing things again, big brother. But let's finish talking about Ginny. You're sure she'll go for this plan?"

Robert nodded, distracted. He swore he heard something like a sob, then the patter of feet fleeing down the hall. He'd bet his fortune it was Lorelai, but that left so many unanswered questions. What would she be doing there? Why did she leave so quickly?

"Ginny's great. I talked to her. Are you sure you didn't hear anything? It sounded like Lorelai."

"Lorelai? Then why didn't she come in?"

"I don't know, but I've got to find out. Will you meet

me later to work on the finishing touches?"

"Sure. Good luck, Robert. And hey, if you see Patricia, can you ask her to order some of that white beer from the Netherlands? I love Aurelia, but this is the worst."

Robert waved a generic response to Philip and tore out of the room and down the hall. When he got to the doors, the guard opened them automatically. Halfway through them, Robert turned around.

"Branson."

He made it a point to know every member of staff, guards especially. Their names, their families. Guarding the palace, working for the crown, it was a noble calling. That didn't mean that was all that made up the men and women who served Aldonia, though.

"Yes, Your Grace?"

"Did Lorelai come through here a minute ago?"

"Yes, Your Grace. Was I supposed to alert you she'd arrived?"

Robert shook his head and waved off Branson. "No, no. She's family. She may come and go as she pleases. Did she leave shortly afterward?"

"She did, Your Grace."

Crap. At least his suspicions were correct. It didn't answer any of the questions rolling around in his mind, though.

"Did she look, um, well, upset?"

"When she left, Your Grace."

What the—? Alarm bells rang in his chest, constricting it and making it hard to breathe. The new information only served to add more questions to the growing list. So, she'd been happy when she arrived? But not when she left? And she hadn't been there long? What could have possibly happened in such a short span of time to upset her?

Everyone at the palace was aware of his plans to surprise her, many actively helping with the planning or execution of the work, so at least he was certain no one she ran into would have been anything but kind, warm.

The whole situation threw him. And really, the only way to get answers to the questions would be to find Lorelai. Ask her himself. It meant putting off hanging the pictures and displaying the final element of the surprise only he and a few staff were aware of, but he had to talk to her.

Something isn't right.

He felt it deep in the part of him that had known what Patricia came to tell him before she'd ever said a word the night his parents died.

"Thanks, Branson. How's Marguerite?"

"She's better, thank you, Your Grace. Your recommendation went a long way in curing her. We're very grateful."

"Good, I'm glad to hear it. Give her my best. Can you point me in the direction Lorelai took off in?"

Branson smiled and nodded toward the north end of the property.

The horses. Of course.

"Thanks, Branson."

"My pleasure, Your Grace. Good luck to you both."

Robert was off again, the tightness in his chest breaking loose with each step. He didn't head north, though, but east. She might have a better working knowledge of his land outside of the property, but she hadn't needed to elude countless guards and heads of staff just for a moment of privacy. No one knew the castle grounds like he did, except maybe his brother.

His shortcut was grown over, thorn bushes snagging him each way he curved and darted around the turns in the path. The pricks stung his skin as they pierced through with a vengeance, but he couldn't slow down. Not when the panic alarms grew louder as he closed in on the north stables.

Muscle memory told him where to go instinctively, so that his mind didn't waver from Lorelai.

As the bushes opened up, the stables came into view.

So did Lorelai, tears streaming down her face as she stalked down the pedestrian path toward her horses.

"Lorelai," he called out. She was mere feet in front of him—with a step he could have her in his arms, wrapped in an embrace. His skin tingled with want, need.

She whirled on him, her eyes mirroring the mix of alarm and pain in his, but of course, hers was directed at him. When she wiped at the rogue tears with her sleeve, part of him cracked, broke irrevocably. He kept failing her, he just didn't know why he had this time.

"Get away from me, Robert. You've made it as clear as you possibly can how you feel about me, and believe me, I've heard you this time. I'm done." She stormed off to the barn, but he stayed at her heels. He wasn't letting this woman out of his sight. Not ever again.

"Lorelai. I've messed up in the past with asking you to be someone you're not. I know that and admit it freely. But I wouldn't make the same mistake twice. Not if I knew it meant I'd lose you."

She paused. A good sign.

But then she just went right back to assembling the tack for what he assumed would be a ride with Billie Jean. Lord, she was as stubborn as anyone he'd ever met.

"You don't know anything about me, Robert. We had a hot month or so in bed, but that's all it was."

That, the lying, he wasn't going to listen to. He placed a hand on hers. She yanked it out from under his like he'd scalded her.

"Now stop right there. We were more than that, and you know it. Pretending otherwise is an insult to how great we were, how great we could be, Lor."

Her gaze fell to the dirt floor of the centuries-old stable. If only he could get her to the new barn, to her new apartment. Show her just how much he knew her.

"Pretending otherwise is the only way I'll make it out of this alive. Now, if you'd please leave me alone so I could take Billie Jean out for a last ride."

"What do you mean, last ride? You have another few days here."

"Not anymore. I'm headed to the airport tonight to go on standby. Gregory arranged it for me."

He *what?* Gregory was in on the surprise reveal of the new facility, a facility Robert had hoped Lorelai would run.

"You can't go, at least not until you tell me what happened. Why did you storm out of the castle?"

That got her attention. She placed the saddle and bridle on the mare and turned slowly to face him.

"Who told you I was there?"

"No one. Branson pointed out where you were headed, but I heard you in the hall. Why didn't you knock? Come in? It's still your home, Lor."

She sneered at him. "Seriously? You wanted me to come in and take part in you telling Philip that the only reason you wanted me to stay was because I was a good mother to Ginny and you didn't want to give that up?"

Now it was Robert's turn to be confused. What was she talking about? He recognized some of the words, but the rest she'd taken completely out of context.

"What are you talking about, Lorelai? We weren't even discussing you. Philip and I were talking about Ginny, and how she would feel about you staying. Philip was concerned she wouldn't like my shared attention, that I should talk to her, but, Lorelai, I already have."

"You said, 'Lorelai's a great mom to Ginny' and that you didn't want to give that up."

Lorelai's chest expanded slowly, then trembled as she exhaled. Why wouldn't she look at him? He kept talking, hoping it would keep her there.

"I don't want to give that up, Lorelai, but you missed all of the context of that comment. I didn't want to give you up just because Ginny acted like a four-year-old. If you'd have stuck around, I was going to add that I would give up your relationship with her if it meant I could keep you in my life. I know you aren't ready to be a mother. But

I'm not ready to live without you."

Soft tears fell on Lorelai's pale-pink sweater, making crimson splotches that added a sense of macabre to the already heavy feeling in the air.

"Robert—" she started, but Billie Jean snorted and tossed her bridle. Lorelai shushed her, but worry etched her face.

"Lorelai, I love you. I'm *in love* with you. I can't tell you how sorry I am that I didn't see you, listen to what you needed. It was purely selfish and won't ever happen again. I can promise you that."

Billie Jean grunted and shimmied around in her stall. She seemed anxious despite the fact that Lorelai took her time with the mare, rubbing her hands over her hair, murmuring to her. Robert patted her on the hindquarter, but she swatted him away with her tail and reared up like she might kick.

"What's wrong with Billie Jean?" he asked.

"I'm not sure. She's been agitated since the fire. I don't know why it seems worse today, though."

"How can I help?"

"I think you should leave, Robert. I hear what you're saying, but right now isn't the time or place." She hopped up in the saddle to a whinny from Billie Jean.

His heart expanded and pressed against his chest, or at least he felt like it did. Really, it shattered, somehow pumping blood to his extremities despite being in a thousand pieces.

"Lorelai," he said. He put his hand on her knee that was now almost eye-level with him. In a split second—faster than he could register, Billie Jean bucked, sending Lorelai rocking forward into her neck. The mare then reared up on her hind legs and keened.

Lorelai clung to the horse's neck, her face bone white, fear set in her wide eyes. She screamed as Billie Jean shook her head, hitting it on the thick wood posts that braced the entrance to the stall.

Robert wasn't sure what to do. He froze, panicked about getting too close, hurting her, or Billie Jean.

"Help," she whispered. "Please help me."

That was all the direction he needed. He backed up and whistled, leading an angry Billie Jean out of the stall where there was less of a chance for her to toss Lorelai into something dangerous. Or worse, toss her to the wood-chip-covered floor underfoot of the enormous beast.

Billie Jean trotted out, her head still swaying side to side.

Good. Now he just needed to get her out of the barn. Most likely Billie Jean felt trapped, understood the danger that faced her last time she'd been enclosed, flames lapping at the edges of her safety.

No matter what happened next, he needed to get the mare—and probably the other horses who'd survived the fire—rehabilitated so this didn't keep happening. Something to worry about when Lorelai was safe. When Billie Jean was contained.

Robert walked backward, careful to keep an eye on the horse and its rider, who looked as terrified as he'd ever seen her. She knew what horses were capable of, so of course she would worry about her own safety. Robert's pulse raced and sweat beaded on his forehead.

When the trio was out of the barn, Billie Jean whinnied and took off like the Devil chased her.

No. Dammit.

Robert raced back in the barn and grabbed the nearest saddle and tack, not caring that they weren't European. He'd figure it out along the way. He just needed to get to Lorelai. And fast.

He threw the ensemble on the back of a gelding whose sign outside the stable door read *Lightning Stick*, hoping to God it wasn't a name mired in irony. He needed lightning and a little luck from the gods to get him to the woman he loved before it was too late.

He wasn't the praying kind, but he found himself

pleading that he could save Lorelai before she was hurt, or worse. He led Lightning Stick out of the barn and in the direction Billie Jean had gone in, yelling at the horse to ride like he'd never ridden before.

Please, Robert whispered to the fall breeze, *please let her be okay.*

CHAPTER THIRTEEN: THE FIX

Lorelai clung to the horse's hair, no longer caring that it wasn't good practice. This was triage, her only thought how she would make it out of this alive, hopefully unscathed. If she did, she would change so much about her life. No more taking it for granted.

Waiting for the right time.

The opportune moment.

The perfect words.

She would seize it all when seizing the nonexistent reins on this runaway horse didn't override all her other senses.

Wind raced around her, whipped her hair in her eyes, her mouth. She didn't dare try to swipe them free of the obstruction to her sight, her breath. Though a competent rider, this scared the daylights out of her, being out of control on an animal that weighed half a ton more than her. She needed both her hands to navigate.

Oh, God. Please let this end soon. One way or another.

At least they were out of the barn. Out here, Lorelai only need worry about hanging on, and that, she could do. In the barn, though, she'd been so scared that Billie Jean would throw her, then trample her as she tried to find a way out of the stall.

She didn't dare look back, but she really hoped Robert was behind her.

He would be. He had to be.

She was as sure of that as she was that she loved him. Though her heart pounded furiously against her chest and adrenaline coursed through her veins, her head was clear.

Horses or not, Lead Huntsman or not, the only things she couldn't live without were Robert and Ginny. Yes, they had some issues to work out, namely his control over her schedule and the fact that travel on behalf of the state wasn't anything that interested her, but she loved him, too. That was clear as a mountain stream to her.

When Billie Jean first bucked in the barn, Lorelai's instinct had been to beg for more time. Time with her brother. With Robert and Ginny.

To pretend she felt otherwise only benefited her ego.

She could swallow her pride and let him love her. Hell, it was all she'd ever wanted from the time she was old enough to want in that way. She just needed the horse to stop, to let her off so she could tell him.

"Billie Jean, I need you to stop. Please," she whispered in the horse's ear.

Like some sort of miracle, Billie Jean slowed to a trot. If Lorelai jumped now, she'd be okay. A little banged up, but she'd survive.

She threw one leg over the saddle, still clinging to the mare's mane until she could find a less rocky patch of terrain.

"That's it, Billie Jean. Just a little slower, hun, and then you and I can take a break, get you some help. You just need to help me first, okay?"

In her befitting way of understanding Lorelai more than most people did, Billie Jean stopped dead in her tracks and let loose a whinny devoid of any angst or fear.

She stopped. Lorelai was free. Her hands trembled as she released the horse's mane. They were cramped, but otherwise okay.

Lorelai slid from the horse's back and fell to her knees. A feral sob escaped her chest as she filled her shaky hands with the dry dirt and small pebbles lining the path.

She was safe. Unharmed.

Billie Jean meandered along the side of the trail, nibbling on dried grass. All evidence of her inner turmoil evaporated, snorts of pleasure replacing the anxious braying from before.

"Good girl," Lorelai said between fits of sobs. "You're my good girl."

When something heavy landed on her shoulder, Lorelai spun around on her knees, fear back with a vengeance.

"Lorelai. Oh, God, Lorelai. Are you hurt? Show me where. I'm so sorry I couldn't catch you."

Lorelai stood, her legs unsteady. She threw her arms around Robert's neck, diving into his warmth. The weather wasn't yet cold, but Lorelai shook from her shoulders to her feet like they were caught in a snowstorm. Even her teeth chattered.

"I'm okay. A little in shock, but I'm fine."

Robert's hands enveloped her, pulled her in tight against him.

Home. He feels like home. Like her future and her past mingled into one perfect person meant only for her. She inhaled the cool air into her chest and her breathing slowed. The aroma of pine and sawdust filled her nostrils, adding to the memories of her past that swirled around her. Why didn't he smell like his normal cologne mixed with cinnamon? Not that she would complain. He was as delectable as usual, maybe more so.

"Lorelai, I'm so glad you're okay. When I thought… When I thought you might—"

"But I didn't. Everything's going to be okay." She stretched up on her toes to touch her lips to his, but when she got there and felt the tremble of his jaw, greed consumed her.

Her mouth closed in on his, her tongue eager to taste

his and tangle with it. He might have smelled like pine and earth, but he tasted like the cinnamon she'd come to associate with him. That and sugar, like he'd been baking before coming to her rescue.

She moaned with pleasure, pressing her pelvis against his. He groaned in response, both of them animalistic in their need for each other.

Lorelai jumped up and wrapped her legs around Robert's waist. His arms encircled her, his fingers tangled in her hair. Her mouth parted, inviting him further inside her. Heat built in her stomach and migrated south when she thought of other ways she wanted this man to explore her. She wanted the hard length of him that was pressed against her stomach to delve inside her depths, fill every inch of her ache for him.

She pulled back, breathless and half crazed with desire.

"What was that?" he asked.

She didn't know. Only that she'd felt something, and that something had overridden her senses. Including her good sense, apparently.

"Thank you for coming to get me."

He ran a hand through hair that had grown longer. Small curls lined his forehead. She liked it. More than liked it, actually.

"You're, uh, you're welcome."

The pause that filled the open air around them was heavy as a winter storm. She could love him all day long, but she couldn't change his mind about his feelings for her.

"I guess you should take me back so I can finish packing, huh?"

"I have something to show you first. Will you come with me?"

Her curiosity was piqued, but not enough to override the spike in lust that screamed inside her. She needed to escape this man who threatened to ruin her plans to leave with her dignity still intact.

"Okay. But it has to be quick."

"Of course." He smiled. Was that a glint of humor she saw etched in his dimples? His eyes seemed awfully bright for a man who'd just rescued a damsel in distress, a damsel who was hightailing it out of the country before she stripped naked in front of him, demanding he sleep with her.

Robert came from behind her and scooped her into his arms. She screamed with surprise. Now that she was safe, all she wanted was to see what this man's strength was capable of. But she'd lost that right, that privilege.

He plopped her down on Lightning Stick's saddle, then went to tie Billie Jean to the nearest elm with her lead rope. He didn't have to say anything for Lorelai to understand they were leaving the horse there, that they'd come back for her when they had a better place to put her. Lorelai hoped the new barn was finished soon so Billie Jean could go home. It wouldn't fix everything, but it would be a place to start.

For someone else to start. God, that stung, the sudden realization that she wouldn't be around to witness the rehabilitation of Billie Jean. And so many other transitions with the horses and stables and hunts.

Could she endure another loss? Another heartbreak? She'd have to when she said goodbye to her horses, when she left them for someone else to help them. Ugh. This was killing her.

She cleared her throat, wishing it would clear away the doubt that crept along the periphery of her thoughts. Was she doing the right thing in leaving? He'd said he loved her. Wasn't that enough?

"So you picked this old trotter to chase after Billie Jean? You must not have wanted me to be safe after all." She tried for light-hearted, but still, the words felt heavy.

"You've misnamed the poor schmuck. He traveled like he was headed to the glue factory. It was borderline pathetic."

Lorelai laughed, feeling the last of the panic and fear evaporate from her system, only to be replaced with a crippling sadness. She would miss this, all of this.

"Yeah, that was my dad. He thought it would be funny to give a horse like that to a pompous old hunter and watch the hilarity ensue. I get how this might not have been the best timing to test that theory out."

"You think? Come on. Let's get out of here."

"Yes, please."

Robert wrapped his arms around Lorelai's waist. God, how she missed his touch, his presence. She was the best version of herself around him. Well, most of the time.

She laid her hands atop his, not worried about being atop Lightning Stick's back. He was calm to a fault, and she couldn't blame all horses for Billie Jean's panic. Heck, she couldn't even really blame Billie Jean for that.

To that line of thinking, though, who would take over the rehabilitation of the frightened horse? There were only a few people she trusted with that responsibility in Europe, even less in Aldonia. Oh, well. It wasn't her problem to solve anymore.

They rode in silence, the day's events weighing down any attempt at banter.

She hadn't had a chance to tell him how she felt, that she loved him, but now that the thrilling events of the afternoon had calmed, she needed to. She couldn't let him think she was leaving because she didn't care for him. Nothing could be further from the truth.

When they sauntered up to the newly rebuilt barn—a trip that took them three times as long on the way back to the castle as hers had taken in the sprint away from it—Lorelai gasped. It looked the same as it always had, before the fire anyway. For a while, it had seemed like Robert was guiding the rebuild toward a more modern approach, but this was better.

So much better.

The wood paneling looked newer, sure, but he'd still

chosen distressed pine, exactly what her father's barn had been constructed with.

"Robert, it's beautiful."

"I'm glad you like it. C'mon. I want to take you through the rest."

He slid off the gelding and took her hand, helping her down as well. Tears brimmed and threatened to fall, but she swallowed hard. Jesus, this was just the outside of the thing—she should probably hold the theatrics for the rest of the tour.

He walked her through the stables and she couldn't believe the similarity to the previous structure. Even the sign that used to hang over the south entrance, *My barn— My rules* had been remade and hung in its same location. She ran her hand along the stall where Billie Jean would live, noting that somehow, some way, the notch in the door where a juvenile Billie Jean had bucked, chipping the panel, was still there.

How the—?

"Your brother told me the story. I made sure we honored her past as much as we could." Robert seemed to sense her amazement.

She swallowed hard and nodded.

"We, um, didn't leave everything the same, though. I had my fire safety team install a state-of-the-art sprinkler system that not only detects a change in temperature, but knows when and how much it should dispense to keep the flames from spreading. To the horses, it would just seem like a light rain."

There was nothing Lorelai could do to stop the tears from falling at that point. It was perfect. Everything just as her father had left it. Everything that mattered, anyway. The rest was even better. She reached for Robert's hand and squeezed it. She didn't have the words to express her gratitude. Plus, even if she did, they'd only come tumbling out of her like a damp, soggy mess. She was blubbering now.

Not her finest moment.

"Are you up for one more?"

Am I? This day had been the strangest in her recent memory, and it just kept getting worse.

Or rather, better. She just didn't know what to make of it. She nodded. She'd be okay, as long as she had him by her side. For as long as she could get him, anyway.

Robert squeezed her hand back and guided her to the stairs that led up to the barn manager's apartment. It had always been in her family, and now that she stood at the precipice, she wasn't sure she wanted to look in. For the first time, it would belong to someone else, and she wasn't sure her heart could handle that with the grace Robert deserved.

Not especially if he'd designed it like the barn—a mirror image to what her father had built when he'd designed the first royal stables. It would hit too close to home to then have to hand it over to a stranger.

They were at the door. Too late to turn back. She inhaled, a sharp breath that stung her lungs with ice.

The heat faded quicker with each day. She'd wasted so many weeks of the hunting season between the fire and before that, shacking up with Robert and Ginny. It might be too late for whomever came in to do much with the hounds, not to mention the traumatized horses, this close to winter. Yet another loss in a season of them.

"Shall we?" he asked. His hand was still wrapped in hers, but he dropped it when she went to reply, only to be a teeth-chattering mess. Instead, he wrapped his arm around her waist and nudged closer to her. With every touch, he made it harder for her to leave.

"I am."

A lie, perhaps, but a necessary one. She needed to rip the Band-Aid. Move on.

When the door swung open, though, she wasn't sure that would be possible.

"What is this?" she asked. Her voice was a whisper, but

it raked along her throat that cinched with pain at the sight in front of her.

"You don't like it?" Robert sounded concerned, but she no longer cared for his feelings. His renovation, though stunning, was too cruel.

She shook her head, the movement costing her greatly. Her neck was tightening up from the ride she'd endured, and the stressed response to the apartment in front of her didn't help anything.

He dropped his arm and moved so that he faced her. His hands sat on her shoulders like anvils, weighing her down.

She couldn't look at him.

She turned her face, a soft sob escaping when her father's table came into view. How dare Robert. That was *hers*. It didn't belong there anymore, it belonged wherever she ended up. Which would be New York.

If the barn was similar to what her father had built, the apartment took that to an eerie level. It might as well have been the same place as before the fire, with only small enough discrepancies that only she would notice. The overstuffed armchair with the same pattern, but sans the claw marks on the oak legs. The original had survived the time nine-year-old Lorelai had snuck a barn kitten into the apartment—not unlike Ginny—and the animal had found every piece of wood offensive. Then there was the table. It was damaged from the fire, but whoever had restored it had made it a work of art. It was seventy percent her father's work, but with purposefully-chosen darker wood to accent the repair. She trailed a finger along the seam that sewed the table of her memory with the one that stood in front of her.

Her pulse quickened and the tears came hot and heavy.

A hand rested on her shoulder. She didn't have the energy to shrug it off.

"Why don't you like it? Did I get something wrong?"

She shook her head. The furniture, the décor, even the

photos on the wall were the same. *How* he'd done it didn't concern her as much as *that* he'd done it.

When her gaze landed on the small wooden figurine above the fireplace, her breath hitched in her chest.

"This is… this is my figurine. From my father." A sob wracked her body, heaving her chest to the point it might break.

"It is. But it's supposed to be a happy surprise. What's wrong, Lor?"

She was confused. She had to be. Because as long as she'd known this man, loved him with every cell in her body, he'd never been intentionally mean to her. Daft, yes, but never cruel.

When she didn't respond, he continued.

"I know you're bent on leaving, but I thought maybe if you had a place to call your own, if the operation was yours—all of it, no strings this time, that maybe you'd stay. It doesn't have to be with me, but just stay, run the show. You've more than earned it. You're the best man for the job, Lor."

She giggled, the sound offensive and inappropriate in the austere silence.

Lorelai stared at Robert like he might suddenly sprout wings and fly away.

"Why are you offering this now?"

"I know it looks bad, like I'm doing it out of guilt, but honestly, Lorelai, if I wasn't so blinded by love before, I would have offered it to you right away. Selfishly, I worried if you ran the hunt, I'd never see you. But you were always the best person for the job. I still love you and I probably always will, but that won't ever get in the way of how I give you my support. I promise. Will you think about it? About the job, I mean? I don't think for a minute you'd consider my other offer to—"

Lorelai closed the two steps between her and Robert and leapt on him, wrapping her legs around him like she had in the field. Her mouth closed over his, and she wasted no time prying his lips open with her tongue, diving in to taste him, explore him. She could have made him wait, maybe even should have, but nothing was going to get between her and what she wanted anymore. Not even her pride.

He didn't seem to mind. His mouth matched her passion, his tongue tangling with hers. His hands cupped her backside, his fingers delicately splayed at the entrance to her sex. She let a gasp escape as he rubbed the place in her that craved him, ached for him over her clothing.

In the spirit of not letting anything come between her and her needs, her clothes had to go. Now.

Robert pulled away, and her mouth felt the loss as acutely as she had the first time they'd kissed in the field. That seemed like years ago.

"Does this mean…?"

"Yes." She cut him off with another kiss, this one more sensual. "I love you, Robert. I always have. It seems a little bit of a waste not to see where it might go."

"So, you'll stay?"

"I will. Yes, I will. You made this place too perfect to leave it to anyone else."

He smiled, the glint of mischief back in his eyes.

"I hoped it would work. Gregory and Philip helped."

"Thank them for me." She brushed her lips over his.

"I will. Later. You're staying—that's all that matters now."

"But I need to know two things before I unpack."

"Anything. I'll tell you anything. I'll give you anything. My world is yours for the taking, Lorelai."

"First, who fixed my father's table? It's perfect. Flawless, even though it was all but rubbish."

"I did. I'm not just a pretty face, you know." He winked at her, the mischief driving her wild. She rarely got to see this side of him. It was different, but still very much Robert in all the ways that counted.

"Well, a rich, pretty face. Oh, and King. You've got a

few good traits, I guess."

He laughed, nuzzling his face in her hair. He growled and ran his tongue along her earlobe, sending chills and fire simultaneously down her spine. He was a freaking magician and she was desperate to learn all of his tricks.

"I want you, Robert," she breathed into his hair.

She no longer cared about her second question. She only wanted to take this man, right there on the table he'd fashioned for her from pure magic and skill.

"I want you, too. But not yet. Ask me your second question."

God, his voice sounded like sex, heavy and deep. Her body almost mutinied, and she almost tore his clothes off then and there. Ugh. She'd best get this over with so she could start enjoying her new job—sleeping with the boss as one of the perks she was looking forward to most.

"Fine. I just need your word that I'll have full control of the hunt and the barn."

"With my whole heart, I mean it, Lor. So long as you consider one more proposal."

She frowned. So help her, if he promised her the world only to yank it out from underneath her, she'd strangle him herself. Prison would be better than Robert's give and take.

But when he bent down on one knee, her breathing stopped altogether. She grew dizzy, small pinholes of light infiltrating her peripheral vision. Finally, in one final push from her body, she gasped for air, taking in the moment while much-needed oxygen flooded her system.

He knelt in front of her, a wooden box identical to the siding on the barn opened in front of him. Inside, a diamond the size of one of the new barn kitten's paws shone bright. It reflected the light from the kitchen, sending small rainbows across her walls. It was such a beautiful sight, it moved her to tears until she grasped why he was there, presenting her with the most stunning piece of jewelry she'd ever seen.

"Oh, my God."

"Lorelai, will you marry me? Be my queen? Leave the country to me—all I need is you to come home to at the end of the day. For the rest of my life."

Yes, she would have screamed if her voice wasn't a traitorous jerk. Instead, she nodded until her breathing regulated and she could whisper, "Yes. Yes, I'll marry you. Oh, my. Are you sure? Is Ginny sure?"

"Will everyone stop assuming I haven't gotten her full permission for this? Of course, she's happy. She loves you as much as I do, Lor. But you don't have to jump into being her mother. She understands it may take some time for you to adjust…"

Lorelai shook her head. "No. I want it all. All of you, including being your wife and her mother." She didn't have time to wait for a response. With a flourish, she was up in Robert's arms, heading for the bedroom. She gasped when he carried her over the threshold.

"This is the one place I made some upgrades, love." The room with its king-sized, four-poster bed, with its skylight and wall of windows—the modern touch she'd seen from the castle—was nothing compared to hearing him call her *love*.

Everything was perfect, down to the three-carat ring she wore, representing the unity of her past and future. Crooking a finger toward Robert, she motioned him to her. She lay back on the satin comforter and lifted her hips, sliding her pants down around her ankles. Removing her top after that, she lay bare for him, her legs spread in invitation.

"Come here, my love. Let me show you how excited I am to be your wife."

"Good God, Lorelai, how I'm going to get anything done with you around is beyond me. I want you so badly."

Robert bent down over Lorelai, using one hand to pull his chambray button-down over his broad shoulders. Shoulders she couldn't wait to run her hands along, the muscles pliant under her touch. His lips peppered Lorelai's earlobe with kisses. Tingles shot across her skin each time his mouth brushed her skin. He lit her on fire, something she hoped never faded.

They spent the next two hours together, each taking control at different times, each doting on the other with equal parts passion and tenderness. Lorelai felt herself sliding further into love with her life, with Robert.

This was what she'd always dreamed of, and it was finally hers for the taking. She wouldn't let it go this time.

Not for anything in the world.

**

Robert breathed in the smell of Lorelai's hair. How could she have done what they'd just done and still smell like vanilla and cinnamon? She was made of his dreams, incarnate.

"The country is going to love you." He circled his arms around her, desperate to keep her close.

"I hope I'm good enough for them."

"You're more than that. You're perfect." He bent down to kiss her, wiping away a stray tear that sat on her flawless skin with his lips. "Besides, how could they have anything but love for an Aldonian woman as queen? The last two have been Georgian or Russian, so you're a shoo-in."

Her laughter shook his chest. God, that sounded good, felt even better. His future wife in his arms, the last of the afternoon sun peeking through the large, open windows he'd had installed on the east and west walls of the apartment. He never wanted Lorelai to miss a sunrise or sunset.

"Well, perfect or not, I'm not sure I'll ever get used to people calling me Queen."

That warmed Robert's chest in the place Marjorie had frozen over in her desperate attempt for the title. Knowing

Lorelai didn't want it made her all the more perfect for the role, for him.

"They won't be at first. Not until you're crowned after our wedding."

"Our *wedding*. Wow. One *yes* changed everything, didn't it?"

"It did, my Imminent Queen."

"Imminent Queen? No *way*." Her face scrunched up like she'd eaten something foul. "That can't be what they call me. It's too… too frilly. Plus, it sounds like I'm about to do something. But what?"

Robert laughed, heavy and loud.

He kissed the top of her head again. Inhaled the smell of pine and vanilla that he'd come to associate with her.

"I'm afraid that's your official title until we're married, my love."

She looked up at him, and in her eyes, he saw reflected everything he'd ever wanted.

"Then let's get married immediately."

"Just so you can carry the title of Queen?"

"Sure. We can say that. We don't want everyone to know I've loved you since the beginning of time. It'll make me seem desperate."

"No, love. I don't want them to know that, either."

Lorelai playfully slugged him on the arm.

"I don't want them to know that I was an idiot until now. I should have noticed you sooner." He meant that with every cell that made him who he was. He'd almost missed out on the best thing to happen to him, to Ginny. That scared him. He pulled her closer to his chest.

"You couldn't have. You weren't ready. It happened exactly as it was supposed to."

He smiled, even though she couldn't see it.

"You're right, love. Like always. And you know I'll never get in the way of your dreams again, right? You'll make a heck of a huntsman, and if I'm being honest, I can't wait to see those riding breeches on you." He winked and pinched her exposed backside. He got half hard with that simple gesture.

Good Lord, how was he supposed to get anything done around this woman?

She blew a raspberry on his chest and threw another playful punch. "You tease, but I look pretty great in my riding crop. Maybe I'll show you just how great later tonight."

"Ooh, I'd like that."

"But in all seriousness, Robert, I wouldn't even consider saying yes to your proposal if I didn't know you'd let me live my own life beside you. I also wouldn't have said yes if I didn't envision being your partner, being by your side when you need me. You just have to give me notice, okay?"

"It's more than okay. It's perfect, like you. How about I call Patricia tomorrow and tell her we can't wait another minute to marry. Get you out of being the Imminent Queen. What's the use of being King if I can't pull a few strings every now and then?"

"I won't argue with that. We're going to live happily ever after, aren't we?"

He pulled back so he could meet her gaze.

"We are, Lorelai. We are. With a sprinkle of adventure if you're up for it."

"Oh, I am."

"Good. Because I have a few ideas of how we can kick things off."

With that, he dipped down and locked his lips with hers, then teased her mouth open with his tongue. His hands slipped beneath the sheets and found her legs parted for him. This wasn't a bad way to start the rest of his life with the woman of his dreams.

Not a bad way at all.

CHAPTER FOURTEEN: THE FUTURE

Robert took in the crowd with a discerning gaze. Women sashayed through the room, their ballgowns brushing the floor, their jewelry reflecting the already elegant lighting in shards and crescents that glittered against the satin-covered walls. The men were dashing in their tuxedos, polished shoes, and slicked coifs. It was an event for the ages. Everyone in attendance would remember being there as long as they lived. Their children would be told of the night.

And if it weren't for Lorelai, none of them would be there. She'd convinced Robert through a magical combination of researched logic and empathy to contact Russia, to work through their issues. She'd given him a fail-proof plan that had gone over better than any of Robert's advisors had thought it would. If he hadn't been the one to broker the deal on behalf of his country, he never would have been able to tell that the two countries were on the verge of war just months prior.

The night was a success because his soon-to-be-wife was as brilliant as she was beautiful. He'd love for her to see the fruits of her labor.

"How is the future Queen? She did quite a job making tonight happen." Robert's advisor, Petre, patted him on the shoulder. Robert couldn't remember the last time he'd seen the man smile, let alone relax. Yet there he was, a martini in hand, a wide grin crinkling the corners of his eyes.

"She did, didn't she? She's perfect, but you know that. She's also brought our hunting operation back up to speed, and dare I say stronger than it was. I hate to admit I was wrong in hiring Simon, but..." Robert shrugged his shoulders.

"I'm glad to hear it. Do you miss her while you're on the road?"

"Terribly, but I know she's working hard for her dreams, for our country while I'm away. Taking care of the princess and training her to take over the barn someday. She's got her role, and I've got mine." Still, the idea of her not being beside him left an ache that only subsided when he was home, with her. With both his ladies.

"And how are you faring without Patricia?"

Robert shook his head. "We're ready to have her back. She deserved the month away—heck she deserves a year off with pay for all she's done for me—but Ginny is ready to start her last year of preschool. That, and I am in desperate need of her corned beef and cabbage. Or anything other than grilled chicken. I feel like I'm wasting away with Lionel."

"Well, you're a saint for sending her. Where did she choose to go?"

"The Turks and Caicos Islands. To an all-inclusive. I don't know that we'll ever get her back with how much fun she's having."

"You've heard from her?" Petre tipped his drink back and swallowed the last of the liquor in his glass. "I don't know if you sent me on a vacation I'd be checking in."

"She sent a postcard. Said she met some woman from

America and might swing by a small town in Idaho on her way home to meet the woman's family."

"Wow. Well, I'm glad she's enjoying herself. I'm looking forward to seeing her when she's back."

Robert took note of the light in Petre's eyes when he talked about Patricia. Something to explore when they were all back at the palace. Lorelai would get a kick out of this.

The trumpets sounded, distracting him from his near full-time thoughts of his future wife.

"Announcing the arrival of Lorelai, Imminent Queen of Aldonia, Duchess of Puruse."

Robert's stomach flipped, his skin tingling like it did each time he heard her name, her voice. He spun around and willed himself not to run to the siren in a red, clinging dress that hugged her curves, curves he knew by touch and sight that were very much on display at that moment.

His future wife. God, he couldn't wait until he could make her his, forever. Just one more week.

Look at her. She was stunning, by far the most beautiful woman in the room. She sauntered over, her hips swaying with the music, her gaze locked to his. A half smile tugged at the corner of her lips.

Heat flooded his abdomen, and on cue, he was half hard in a way only she could do to him. If he didn't check himself, he'd be at full mast there for all the world to see. What a way to usher in a new peace with Russia.

Christ.

"What are you doing here?" he asked as she sidled up beside him, tucking her arm in his. He inhaled the unmistakable scent of vanilla and pine, dizzy with desire for this woman who kept on surprising him.

"Is that any way to greet your future wife? The Imminent Queen of Aldonia?" She winked and Robert felt his slacks grow tighter around his waist. He chuckled at the tone she used when calling herself the Imminent Queen. She'd told him when she'd first been addressed as

Imminent Queen that she found it hysterical. Not to mention more than a little ironic, given their history together.

But he felt differently. This was his future, tied directly to his past. Nothing about it was funny, especially the fact that he'd almost lost her because of his own stupidity. All he felt was supreme gratitude.

"The dress is stunning. Every other woman here is jealous, my love."

When her cheeks turned a deeper shade of pink than the dress on the woman behind them, Robert smiled. He loved that he had that effect on her and hoped it would never fade.

"My future husband has good taste." She winked, and the bulge in his pants grew.

He hoped that never faded, either—the visceral way his body reacted to the woman he loved more with each day that passed.

"I'd like to meet this amazing fellow." He attempted a wink back, but all it did was serve to elicit a laugh from Lorelai. He'd never been good at that sort of thing. He thanked his lucky stars she loved him in spite of this and an array of other faults he was aware he had.

"I'm not sure you would. He's arrogant and has a hard time sharing his feelings. Plus, he's far better looking than you." Her smile lit up the room. She was befitting of royalty, but more than that, she was the perfect fit for him.

"Is that so?" He pulled her in close and placed a hand just above the perfect curve of her backside. She gasped but kept control of her calm. She was getting the hang of this. That made him happier than anything else, the ease with which she'd taken on her new roles as huntsman, mother, and future queen. Soon, she would be his wife, and that thrilled him to no end.

"It is."

"Then why would you bother to marry such a bore?"

"I love him anyway. He keeps my life exciting."

"He loves you, too. More than you'll ever know."

She smiled up through thick lashes.

Robert drew her chin up to his. He kissed her long and hard, his future wrapped up in the promise his lips made to hers. Whatever else he did in his life, loving this woman would be his greatest adventure yet.

He couldn't wait.

THE END

SNEAK PEEK AT THE THIRD BOOK: REUNITING WITH HER PRINCE

Prologue: Two Years Earlier

I'm taking him home with me tonight.

It was Lissa's first thought when she laid eyes on the stranger across the teak wood bar. Her second thought wasn't quite so innocent. As if to punctuate her desire, a loud clap of thunder boomed and the air vibrated within the small space. A storm was imminent in more ways than one.

He mimed a shiver and smiled back at her—totally not innocent, either—then nodded toward a table by the entrance, his grin an eager invitation.

"Nope," she mouthed, curling her finger in an invitation of her own, *come here.*

He smiled and shrugged then started toward her, his saunter promising fun. And in the nick of time, too. Had it really been almost a full month since she'd left everything behind and bought a ticket to the one place no one would recognize her?

One month. Too short a time to forget the hell awaiting her back home, but an infinity to live without satisfying certain… *needs*. Needs that, thanks to her parents and their helicoptering, she'd ignored too long.

Her cell buzzed on the hardwood bar top. *Crap. Her mother. Again.*

It figured, didn't it? Her mother always did have an eerie ability to interfere in her life, particularly when things were about to get good. Interfering only to ruin them, of course.

"Get you something else?" the bartender asked.

"No, thanks. I'm waiting for someone." *Someone tall, dark, and handsome and only half a bar from her.*

Which meant she definitely did not have time for her mother, father, or anyone not drinking martinis on the beach with her. She turned the buzzing phone off and flipped it over, her mother's voice already too loud in her head.

You have to do this for us, darling.

Surely, you wouldn't abandon us in our time of greatest need, would you? Could you?

She shuddered. How was it always *her* job to fix the problems her parents got themselves into?

Because Nora's death left that responsibility to you, her overeager subconscious chimed in. Another tremor coursed through her as she considered this loss on top of all the others.

She waved the bartender over. "I changed my mind. I'll have another."

She stole a glance at her Hermes watch even though she knew the exact amount of time she had left. Only four days of freedom. Not near enough. Urgency tickled her throat. She attempted to squelch it with a healthy gulp of her refreshed martini, but it barely made a dent.

She'd be home in less than a week. They could talk then.

The handsome stranger moved toward her, his predatory gaze pinned to hers. He still spoke to whoever was on the phone, but they held a fraction of his interest.

His focus was *her. And so the hunted became the hunter.* Fine. She could give him that. As long as she got to feed.

"Sorry," he mouthed.

She shook her head. "No biggie. I'm not going anywhere," she whispered.

His smile lit up the dark bar and simultaneously sent a chill racing down her skin.

"*Sí, claro. No quiero nada sin...* certain assurances," he said into the phone, extending his hand for her to take.

Well, if that voice wasn't just as sexy as the man using it, she'd fly home right then.

"Hi. I'm—" he started but then growled into the phone. "*No, absolutamente no.*"

He took her hand in his and kissed the top of it. *Good grief. This man was sex in sandals.* Adding to her warmth, a small flicker of desire ignited when she caught his gaze, a piercing stare searing her with liquid blue heat. Those crystal azure eyes... the way they glowed as if made of the stars and sea. He kept her hand in his, rubbing circles on the pad of her palm while he nodded into the phone like the person on the other end could see him.

Hmmmm. He was adorable. Another rub she could feel in her bones. *And interested.*

"I'm Gael," he whispered, covering the receiver with his hand. "Sorry. Family." He pointed to the phone and she held her own up, boasting 23 missed texts and two missed calls on her home screen.

"That's why I don't answer," she whispered back conspiratorially.

CHECK OUT THE FIRST BOOK IN AN ALDONIA ROYALS SERIES: *AN HEIR FOR THE SECRET PRINCE*

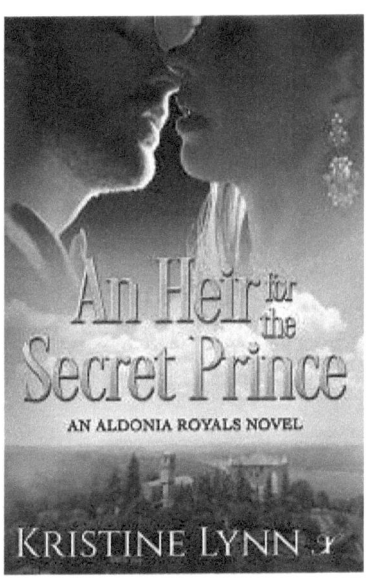

Okay, who invited the journalist?

Philip, advisor to the Prince of Aldonia, is livid when he discovers someone invited a nosy reporter to the palace to write a salacious story about the royal family. The problem is, the more she digs into their pasts, the more she will find out about him—and his private life is none of her damn business. Which is why no one is more shocked than him when, on a whim, he asks her to stay on as his guest.

Aurelia is only certain of two things when she meets Philip on assignment in Aldonia: he's hot as melted sin on a cracker and he's hiding something. Too bad he's NOT the story she's there for. However, that won't stop her from finding out just why he's so reclusive—and tempting.

However, when their growing attraction takes an unexpected turn, Philip may be forced to share his darkest secrets with Aurelia—secrets that will change her life. Will their new relationship be strong enough to overcome the adversity these revelations bring?

EXCERPT:

The truth was, Aurelia didn't care in the least about Prince Gregory or his fortune. He was a story, plain and simple. A means to an end that came with a week abroad on assignment in a place that served dang good wine and hors d'oeuvres.

When one of the women cackled, a high-pitched sound not unlike the hyenas from The Lion King, Aurelia let the giggle escape. It was louder than the noise from the idle conversations, and a few heads turned to look at her.

"Ms. Beck?"

Aurelia choked on her wine as she spun around to face the owner of the deep, sexy voice behind her, sloshing a good deal of what was left in her glass on his shoes in the process. Her heels caught on the long hem of her dress and she nearly toppled over.

Instead, strong hands wrapped around her, locking her in place. Her hand not holding the crystal stemware was pressed against a solid wall of muscled flesh, steadying herself.

"Crap," she muttered, looking down at the shiny black loafers that now had a third of her Merlot on them, patting the chest of the man who'd saved her from eating concrete. "I'm terribly sorry. I was waiting to speak with," she started, her arm flailing behind her in an errant attempt to point out the Prince, but her words—usually her specialty—stuck in her throat.

There, in front of her, his hands still gripping her bare arms, was the most breathtakingly beautiful man she'd ever seen.

Goosebumps erupted over her skin and heat flushed her cheeks.

Good God above.

AVAILABLE WHERE ALL BOOKS ARE SOLD. BUY A COPY FOR YOURSELF!

ACKNOWLEDGEMENTS

This book was so much fun to write because I had the incredible Meghan Moran Wilson to show me around actual hunting stables and to talk me through the inner workings of a hunting operation. Without her, this book would be far less authentic and interesting.

I'd like to thank my colleagues and friends who support this writing journey I'm on. Erica and Stacy especially; you two are next and I can't wait to be at your first book signings!

To my mom and dad, thank you for reading every book and listening to countless ideas for the new ones. Your support and love is the ground beneath my feet.

To my daughter, who writes her own novels beside me reminding me that imagination is something to be cherished and developed. I love talking shop with you, Beanie.

To my writing/critique partners, Anna and Kate, who champion my work and are always willing to talk about books and characters and everything romance. You two are the best, and I can't wait to see your books on shelves.

Finally, to my readers, thank you. I hope you enjoyed book one in this series and that this sequel does your questions justice. You're the reason I love what I do, the proof that love really does make the world go 'round.

ABOUT THE AUTHOR

Kristine Lynn is the author of the *Treasure Valley* and *Secret Prince* romance series, as well as the linked collection of short stories, *Shrapnel*. When she's not writing, she's teaching college students in Arizona and enjoying the Southwest with her husband, daughter, puppy, and three-quarters of a desert tortoise. To connect with Kristine (who also writes under Kama O'Connor), you can email her at kristinelynnauthor@gmail.com or follow her on social media.

Twitter: @kristinelauthor
Facebook: @kristinelynnauthor
Goodreads:
https://www.goodreads.com/user/show/19811168-kama-o-connor
Website:
https://kristinelynn.wixsite.com/author/about